Love is Not a Dirty Word

Love is Not a Dirty Word
and Other Stories

John Wegner

LAMAR UNIVERSITY press

ISBN: 978-0-9915321-6-2
Library of Congress Control Number: 2015931103

Manufactured in the United States of America

Lamar University Press
Beaumont, Texas

For Lana, Jordan, and Clay

Fiction from Lamar University Press

Terry Dalrymple, *Love Stories (Sort Of)*
Gerald Duff, *Memphis Mojo*
Gretchen Johnson, *The Joy of Deception*
Christopher Linforth, *When You Find Us We Will Be Gone*
Tom Mack and Andrew Geyer, editors, *A Shared Voice*
Harold Raley, *Louisiana Rogue*
Jim Sanderson, *Trashy Behavior*
Jan Seale, *Appearances*
Melvin Sterne, *The Number You Have Reached*
Robert Wexelblatt, *The Artist Wears Rough Clothing*

For more information about these and other books, go to
www.LamarUniversityPress.Org

Acknowledgments

I would like to thank Jerry Craven for his editing expertise and for getting these stories to print. Terry Dalrymple was gracious enough to read these in their early form and offer encouraging words and important comments. I learn something about writing every time these two guys offer a comment. Like most writers, I extend a special thanks to my parents and sister for teaching me that stories matter. While none of these stories are biographical, Jordan and Clay deserve credit for at least one of the stories and a few lines in some others, but special thanks to Lana. She read every story more than once and her comments, suggestions, and questions helped more than she'll ever realize.

Some stories in this collection originally appeared in the following journals:

Concho River Review
Journal of American Studies Association of Texas
New Texas
SNReview

CONTENTS

All Beat to Hell

I was living in some graduate student dorms in Denton, about two semesters away from a PhD in Chemical Engineering, when I saw Davey Williams' picture on the front page of the *Dallas Morning News*. It was the kind of story I normally skip—"Cop Killer Gunned Down"—but the image caught my eye. Face down in a pool of blood, a half smile rose from the maroon puddle like a demented drama mask. His right leg was bent toward his chest almost in mid-stride, and his left arm extended to a gun just out of reach. The periphery of the photo showed police and paramedics rushing inside the convenience store, but the dead body held center stage. His eye was half opened as if the camera's flash blinded him for a moment, but I kept looking at the mouth and I could hear his voice from a summer I tried not to think about often.

It's 1985 in the Heritage Oaks Mobile Home Park and the Saturday after school let out for the summer. Colton, Davey, and I had spent most of the morning standing around telling jokes and talking shit—trying to sound tough and more hardened than we felt. We were sixteen at the time, but Colton's birthday was the next week and his dad was taking him to look at a truck that afternoon. Nothing new or fancy, but an engine with four wheels attached was better than what any of us had at the time. Back then, or at least in the neighborhood where we grew up, everyone had more drivers than cars. Colton and I both had a license, but we shared vehicles with our families and parents got first dibs. I didn't get a car to myself until I was a senior, and even then I had to pay for half of it.

Colton and I had been best friends since the first grade. We played in the same Little League, on the same Pop Warner football team, and in the local YMCA basketball league. I can't remember many days we didn't

1

walk home from school together. In high school, we both played football and basketball, but Colton opted out of baseball, and I was cut right before the season started. I wasn't too bummed since it meant we could keep working out together after school. I think my parents were happy they didn't have to buy any more cleats and gloves.

Davey was another story. He and his mom had moved in when we were still in junior high. He didn't play sports, have a license, and wasn't involved in anything, but he was around when Colton and I finished football or basketball practice. I guess we were kind of his extra-curricular activity. My parents weren't all that happy about Davey being in the mix, but my dad told me I was old enough to screw up on my own.

Colton was popular and a damn good football player. He moved up to varsity as a freshman, starting some games at middle linebacker toward the end of the season, and he made all-state as a sophomore. Coach Webster told him in May that UT and A&M had already called for next year's schedule, and I'll admit that I hoped to ride his coattails. The way I figured, playing varsity football and getting a set of wheels wasn't going to hurt his chances with the girls, and I wanted to be there to meet whoever he didn't like. I had kissed a few girls already, and I'd even felt Cindy Cochran's left tit over the Christmas break, but not many girls were interested in a kid from a trailer park with no car. My moment with Cindy was worth bragging about in the locker room, but she was wearing a wool sweater and a bra with enough padding to protect her from a front end collision much less a boy's hand. With Colton's new truck, though, I had visions of paradise by the dashboard lights, or something like that.

That summer morning in 1985, Davey had just finished telling us this nasty Andrew Dice Clay joke. He had stolen one of his mom's cigarettes to use as a prop and he had the clipped, Jersey accent down pat. Colton was leaning on his dad's truck when he took the cigarette, grabbed the lighter from Davey's hand, and lit the smoke. He breathed out pretty quick, and I don't care what they say in those educational movies, he looked like a sixteen-year-old Bruce Willis. Just say no, my ass.

It was his first cigarette of the summer but not his last. He burned that thing to the filter and flicked it out to the road.

"Nobody likes a litterbug. Even in a dump like this."

We turned to look across the street. Lydia Stevens was sitting on her parent's Toyota Corolla. Orangeish with rusted bumpers and dents in odd places, it was all beat to hell my dad had said one morning. "You guys must think you're pretty tough—using grownup words and all." She straightened her legs and rested her hands slightly behind her body, pulling her t-shirt tightly across her chest. "Just because you live in a trailer park doesn't mean you have to act like white trash." She slid off the car and walked to her door, looking like she might say something else, but she shook her head and walked inside.

Lydia Stevens.

I could walk past most people I graduated with and not know them, but there are still days I see Lydia in strangers on the street. The way her hair moved, the wry smile, her eyes probing and twinkling as she laughed. I smiled as I stood up from Davey's picture in the paper to pull my past off the shelf. Twenty-eight years of mementos in one u-haul box.

My parents moved to Florida last year, a reward for years of frugal living and hard work. My dad, unknown to me, had taken night classes for the last fifteen years and he graduated in the spring. When he did, he told me, the job market had "opened up like a baby's mouth looking for its momma's teat. All of a sudden I was this guy with down and dirty real world experience plus that magic piece of paper." He shook his head in wonder at the crazy ways of the world. "I'm not any smarter than I was last year, but damned if I'm going to let anybody know that."

My mom told me over Christmas to get anything I wanted before it got "sold, donated, or dumped." They were headed to Destin June 1st and on June 2nd my mom was going to "by god have some decent furniture for once in my life."

I couldn't tell if she was happier about getting new stuff or not having to take the knicked and chipped things we already owned. When you're poor, she once told me, about the only thing worth keeping are your memories, and even some of them you would donate or throw away if you could.

"Don't let anyone fool you," she added when I asked why they weren't taking any of the furniture they had inherited from her mother. "An antique is someone's trash you paid to bring into your house."

We weren't a family prone to sentimentality. As I looked in the box, I saw a ribbon or two, some photos of Colton and me, and a few other reminders of my childhood. Sitting underneath everything else, tucked into a yearbook I never opened, was a note from Lydia the day she moved. I unfold the paper and I'm sixteen again, walking across the street to talk to Colton and Davey.

The morning Davey told his Andrew Dice Clay joke, I had seen Lydia, but I played it cool. A nod in her direction, what I hoped was a knowing look that showed my maturity. She had long, shiny black hair and every time I saw her she wore blue jeans and a tight fitting t-shirt. I was pretty sure I'd be able to feel her tit even if she did wear a sweater. She also had this way of smiling that made you think she knew something. About you, the world, things beyond that moment.

Today, at 28, I would call her eyes mesmerizing. At 16, going on 17 back in the summer of 1985, I got lost when I looked at those deep pools of color. The few times we had crossed paths, she talked and I stammered, grunted, and sounded like an ape learning sign language at the research lab. Hell, I had a hard enough time holding a conversation with any girl much less one as pretty as her, but each time I looked in her eyes I could see a world that didn't mirror the trailer park. Not that I spent a lot of time looking into girl's eyes at that age, but Lydia's seemed calm and alive and concerned with more than the next party or who might be popular. I could tell she wasn't destined to live in a house on wheels for long.

"What a bitch," Davey said as he kicked a rock and nodded toward Lydia's trailer. "White trash my ass."

"Shut up, Davey." Colton walked out to pick up the cigarette. "I'm goin' in for a while. I'll give you guys a call when we get back from lookin' at that truck."

That summer started about like we expected. Colton's parents bought him a 1970 Chevy truck, a set of tools, and a Chilton's Service Manual. The previous owner had driven the hell out of that truck, but the straight six under the hood could still growl out on the open road.

Those first couple of weeks, the three of us piled in damn near every night. I rode shotgun and Davey sat in the middle fiddling with the radio. Weekdays nothing was ever going on, but with the windows down and the radio playing, we didn't need any place to go. On Fridays and Saturdays things picked up, and we would find someone's older brother willing to buy us a twelve pack or a bottle of gin. We cruised, had a few drinks, and found

ourselves at whatever party someone might be having. Colton knew everyone in town and Davey and I went along for the ride. We didn't exactly
have to beat the girls away with a stick or anything but the days passed.

It was a Saturday night in early July when Pamela Schultz had her
big summer party. Pamela was a year older than us and one of those rich
kids at school. Every year her parents would go on a two-week cruise to
Mexico or Italy, and the last two summers she showed up at the Safeway
parking lot, announcing that the party was at her house. There was a kind
of democratic hedonism in her invitation, and anyone who could get there
without a parent dropping them off or picking them up was invited.

When we pulled up, there were cars everywhere. She lived outside
town in Butler Farms on about ten acres in a house so big my dad saw it
one time and wondered if the maids got travel expenses getting from one
end to the other. When he saw the house, Davey told us it looked like "a
fucking hotel. All three of our trailers would fit in the top floor."

Colton shook his head and finished his beer.

"Alright ladies. I'm goin' in to the circus. It's almost 10:00 and Billy's
gotta be home at midnight. I figure if we leave here about 11:45, I can get
him home on time. And Davey, if you're not here at 11:45, you better hope
somebody else can drive your sorry ass home. If not, we live thataway." He
made a vague motion toward Heritage Oaks.

Once we got inside, Colton wandered off to talk to some guys on the
football team, and Davey went looking "for any lonely chicks who might
need some lovin'." I made my way to the kitchen where Tommy Figaro told
us there were some kegs and "Cindy's in there. Wearin' a t-shirt tonight."
He reached out and grabbed my chest, squeezing and making sounds only
a high school guy being a dumb ass could make.

The kegs were there, but Suzie and her t-shirt had already wandered
off. I stood around talking to a few guys before looking at some pictures
of Pamela and her parents in museums, on beaches, near some ruins—they
had time to live, the money to capture it on film, and plenty of space to
store their memories. I didn't notice Lydia until she was right next to me.
She had a cup in each hand.

"Hey, trailer trash. I didn't know they let your kind in. Pretty
ridiculous, isn't it?" She nodded at the photos. "We can't afford gas to get
to Krogers some days and Pamela's in," she leaned close to a picture,

"Palenque." She turned from the wall and looked toward two floor speakers blasting Madonna's "Like a Virgin," a song that hit too close to home for my taste. "Ughh. I hate this song. Get a refill or grab a straw for that beer you're nursing and let's go for a walk." She touched her shoulder to my arm as she finished her sentence and started walking toward the door.

Lydia was standing near the rail overlooking the back yard when I caught up with her. She looked at me and then out to the yard. "Know the difference between a deck and a porch? What it's attached to. God, someone should unplug those speakers or find some decent music." She stepped past me and headed down into the dark.

We hadn't said anything since we walked off the deck when Lydia turned and handed me one of the beers. Walking behind her, I tried to keep my eyes on her shoulders, but I was 17 so you can guess how well that went. She had on black tights and a long, sleeveless gray sweatshirt that hung mid-thigh and didn't do much to hide her curves.

We reached the fence at the edge of the Schultz's property and Lydia sat down with her back against a fence post. She patted the ground next to her. I figured silence was the best way to avoid making an ass out of myself so I was going to let her talk and play the strong, silent type. Unfortunately, my mouth works independently of my brain.

"So, will you be a junior or senior next year?" In my fantasy conversation, she asks me some deep, philosophical question, and I offer up a romantic, yet witty comment as she reaches for my hand and draws me to her body.

In real life, I spoke first and asked the obvious.

"Who knows. I think I'm halfway between being a junior and a senior. When we lived in El Paso, I skipped the second grade, but we move around a lot and I miss school all the time. My dad's sort of in between jobs. If we're still here, my mom will take my transcripts to the school and they'll tell us what grade I'm in." She took a drink and looked up at the sky. "We haven't been staying around many places very long lately." She sighed. "But enough about me. What brings you out on a night as fine as this? This doesn't strike me as the kind of party folks from Heritage Oaks normally attend."

"Pamela lets about anyone come to her parties. Anyway, she would have invited Colton. They aren't friends, but he's pretty popular." I tried to think of something, anything, to say that might sound less lame. "So, how did you hear about the party? I don't ever see you go anywhere."

"Well, Billy, I declare that almost sounds rude." She did this fake southern accent and put her hand up against her chest. "After my parents are asleep, I get the keys and go driving. Not that they'd care anyway." She paused, took a long drink, and set her empty cup down. "I drive out this direction all the time late at night. There's something stable about big houses sitting on land. Sometimes I come out here and park. Lights will come on late at night as people move around, go to the bathroom, get a snack. People in these houses have a peace of mind that only money can bring. Other times, I get in the car and dream of driving and not coming back. These kids living out here have nothing to lose in this world because someone, or someone's wallet, will always be there to pick them up or bail them out. It must be nice."

We sat and finished the last of the beer. Her mom worked as a secretary at a salvage yard, she told me, but that's all she said about her family. Mostly, she talked about places she had lived and other places she wanted to go. I tried to listen but when I looked at her, I would notice her eyes, the fullness of her lips. At one point, I found myself staring at her neck, slender and graceful, imagining how I would kiss her collarbone, her ear lobe, and then her lips.

She stopped talking and snapped her fingers in front of my face. "You look like you have something on your mind," she said with a wry smile. Her eyes sparkled and she pulled her hair off her neck, before she started laughing softly.

I looked across the yard, embarrassed by my thoughts. She put her hand on my leg, apologized for being mean and leaned over and kissed me, softly brushing her lips against mine. I thought she was a lot of things, but mean wasn't one of them.

Maybe it was the beer or the quiet night, but Lydia and I sat there talking and for that brief moment, I stopped being a nervous little twit, as Colton called me one night after he saw me with Leslie McNulty earlier that summer. I was sitting there with the most beautiful girl in school, but it was probably the longest stretch in my high school years when I didn't think about sex. I told her about Colton and Davey, school, football, anything I could think of to keep her there with me.

"What about your mom and dad, Billy? They seem pretty normal. I don't hear them yelling all that much, at least."

"My mom and dad work hard trying to cover the bills. They both finished high school, but neither one could afford college so they push me pretty hard—I have to study every day after school, or at least I have to go in my room after school and pretend to study. It's kind of a pain in the ass, but not as big a pain as doing bad. Make a *C* and I get the belt."

"At least they care. I've been signing my own report cards since sixth grade."

Lydia looked up at the sky and pointed. "When I was little my dad used stand behind me with his arms around my shoulders, pull me real close, and whisper stories in my ear about cities on other planets and palaces filled with riches, food, and beautiful people. The bad guys were always easy to see and the good guys never got beat. He would point at a star and say, 'Have I ever told you about the little girl who saved all the ducks,' or cats, or whatever animal was on his mind that day? I realized as I got older, he was retelling stories from various t.v. shows—*Battlestar Galactica*, *Dr. Who*, *Star Trek*—but I didn't care because there was always a happy ending. The ducks weren't dead, he would tell me, just hidden in a cave with diamonds and emeralds on the wall. His arms were warm and his hands were rough from work. Then the stories changed somehow. His hands got softer, and he forgot how the stories ended."

I had been looking up, trying to find the star when Lydia stopped talking. When I looked at her, she was staring at her lap and shaking her head, trying to erase the memory somehow.

"That seems like so long ago." Her voice cracked a little. "Happiness is a fucking illusion, my friend." She was crying, but working hard to hold back the tears. I touched her shoulder. It was a tentative pat like I'd seen my dad offer my mom one night. The table was covered with papers, bills I guess. When my parents saw me watching, my dad leaned over and whispered something in my mom's ear as she wiped her eyes. He picked up the papers, and my mom hugged me as she walked down to their bedroom.

I rubbed my hand on Lydia's shoulder and scooted closer to her. She leaned into me and I put my arm around her.

"Well, shit, Billy. Not the rockin' good time you were lookin' for tonight, huh? Sorry about that unfortunate little intrusion from the past." Lydia sat up straight and rubbed her hands through her hair, wiped her eyes. "I'll bet your friends are wondering if you got lucky and here you sit with me crying on your shoulder." She stood up and held her hands out to me. "You've been sweet."

"This has been fun for me." It was a stupid thing to say, but, hell, I was 17 and confused, still hoping for one more kiss before the night ended. As she offered her hand, I saw her watch. "Lydia, what time is it? I don't own a watch." I held my wrists up as proof.

"It's 12:13 on the nose. Do you have a hot date or something?"

"Oh shit." I jumped up. "I'm supposed to be home by midnight or my ass is grass. Colton's probably waiting at the truck." I didn't know what love was, but I was pretty sure I could sit by a fence holding Lydia every minute of my life if she would let me but I also didn't want to get in trouble at home.

"Listen, Lydia, I've got to find Colton." I was ready to race off when she grabbed my hand.

"Chill out. I have a car, remember? If Colton's gone, I can give you a ride. I know where you live."

We started walking around the house toward the front. "Do your parents stay up waiting?"

"I know they don't stay up, but I don't know if they come check in on me at some certain time. I've never been late."

Lydia laughed. "Aren't we the little saint. It looks like he's still here. There's his truck." She pointed. "And there he is."

When we got there, he and Davey were sitting on the tail-gate. Davey saw us first and he hit Colton's shoulder and pointed.

Davey spoke first. "Dude, your dad's gonna to beat the shit outta you." He pointed his finger at me and then smiled at Lydia. "Hey, Lydia. I didn't know you were here."

"Davey, Colton." Lydia held out her hand. Davey looked at her. Colton put his cigarette in his mouth and shook her hand, nodded and looked at me. "Billy, we better get goin'. We can get you home by 12:45. Quicker if we're lucky. Maybe we need to buy you a watch for your birthday."

"Dude," he looked at Colton. "You comin' back after you take him home? I've been making time with this little freshman in there. If you're comin' back, I'm gonna head in there before someone else pops her cherry."

"Jesus, Davey," Colton stood up. "Come on Billy. I'll run you home and then come back for lover boy here."

Davey stood up and turned to go back to the party.

"No need to worry about Billy," Lydia said as she put her arm through mine. "The world needs more 15-year-old cherries popped by guys like Davey." Lydia started walking off before Davey could say anything. "You boys go back to your party, and I'll take Billy home."

I shrugged and smiled with what Colton would describe later that summer as a shit-eatin' grin.

When I went outside the next morning, closer to afternoon really, Davey and Colton were already standing around talking about the night before. They had stayed until around 3:30 and were telling stories about guys throwing up in the bushes, on the couch, "damn near everywhere," Colton said.

Davey told us he walked into Pamela's parent's room and watched two kids fucking, but that was as close as he got to getting laid. "What about you, big dog. Did you get your rocks off with old Lydia last night?"

"Nah. I jumped out the minute we pulled in." I didn't mention that I slept in my shirt so I could smell Lydia's perfume and imagine her head on my shoulder.

"Maybe you should go on over this mornin' and give her a big ol' breakfast sausage," Colton grinned at me as he took a drink of some water. Before I could answer, he turned to Davey. "So, Davey, what was the highlight of your night. Other than pullin' your pud watching some other dude have sex?"

"Kiss my ass. Closer than you got to any pussy last night. I'll tell you what. I met up with Jimmy Frist. Know that dude? He's dealing—ecstacy, joints, small time stuff. Pulled in a couple hundred bucks last night. Those rich kids love to party. Told me he could use a partner. Easy money."

Colton finished his drink. "Don't be a dumbass, Davey. You can fuck up your life any number of ways, but running with Frist is about the worst one."

That was one of the last mornings I remember us hanging out together. Colton and I still worked out every day, but I hooked up with Lydia about every night the rest of the summer. The only time we saw Davey was early in the morning getting out of Jimmy Frist's '68 Chevy Nova. Frist had dropped a 350 big block into that car during shop class the year before, and he finished cherrying it out over the summer. Business was, clearly, pretty good.

In the fall, Colton was living up to expectations on the football field. I started at cornerback on varsity, but it was pretty obvious I was better in the classroom than covering wide receivers. Lydia had enough credits from past schools to come in as a senior, but she dated me anyway. She had plenty of other offers, but I think she liked my awkward innocence.

Lord knows, I was plenty clumsy on the occasions when we would make out, but we spent most of our nights driving around town or lying on the hood of her parent's car looking at the stars. Lydia had dreams, places she wanted to go, and they were infectious. Talking to her that fall, I realized there was a world beyond Heritage Oaks.

We saw less and less of Davey at school. My parents were, I'm sure, worried about Lydia and me running around so much, but more than anything my dad told me years later, they were happy I wasn't anywhere near Davey.

It was December 20th—I remember because we had started Christmas break—when I beat the shit out of Davey. The party was at Elizabeth Nutter's house, less organized than Pamela's, but still out in Butler Farms. When Lydia and I got there, Colton and Davey were talking and from a distance it looked like old times. We walked over in time to hear Colton tell Davey to "get the fuck away from me with that shit." So much for the good old days, I thought.

Davey saw us. "Dude. Old times. The three amigos back together again, and here's little Ms. Lydia Stevens. Hangin' with the trailer trash these days?" He said it in a voice that only someone stoned can use, turning her name into about four syllables. There was something lurking in his voice that put me on edge.

"Hey, Colton. Davey."

Davey looked thinner and hollow—someone who needed to say no more often.

"Davey's trying to sell me some of this shit he and Frist picked up in Houston. He's offering his friends a discount," Colton pointed toward Jimmy Frist as he talked. Jimmy had been having much better luck with Elizabeth and her friends. They were giggling but I could see money in her hand.

"Aw, come on Colton. Shit. If you don't want any of the hard stuff, how about a joint? Hell, half the football team's in the back yard lightin' up right now." He looked at Lydia, his eyes darting back and forth. His sunglasses were on top of his head, but he squinted like he was standing outside in the sun. I saw him smirk and he looked right at me.

"Lydia, I can get you into some of this. Make you feel real good." He sidled up next to me and put his arm on my shoulder. "Come on, Billy, buy Lydia a couple of these." He leaned in closer, holding out two white pills, but he didn't whisper and he looked right at her—"Help her relax a little, if you know what I mean."

Colton grabbed his shirt and got between us. "Leave him alone Davey. What the fuck happened to you?" He shoved Davey away.

Jimmy started walking over and some of the other people turned to watch. I heard someone from across the room yell, "I want to see some bones thrown. Kick his ass, Colton."

Davey stumbled, stuck his middle finger up in the air, and waved Jimmy away as regained his balance.

"Yo, yo, yo." He held his hands up to Colton. "Talking to my man Billy here and he don't need your help or protection." His voice got hard, older than 17 somehow. He looked at Lydia again but started talking to me. "I know you don't have any money, Billy-boy, bein' trailer trash and all, but we can work out a deal." He reached down, grabbed his crotch with one hand and pointed at Lydia with the other. "Me and Lydia can head up to Elizabeth's room for a few minutes..."

I started swinging before he finished. The crunch surprised me, but even today I can see the blood explode from his nose like red water from a hose when I hit him the second time. He went down with his hands over his face and tried to curl up into a ball, but I kept hitting him, straddling his stomach, grabbing his hair with one hand, swinging with the other. The blood spurted from his nose and mouth until his face was speckled red and white. When Colton pulled me off and carried me outside, the knuckles on my right hand looked like a fat candy cane. I started crying as I bent down to wipe my hands on the grass, but the blood in the creases of my knuckles wouldn't come out and I could feel my hands cooling off and starting to throb.

Lydia had my face in her hands trying to calm me down. She took my hands and turned to Colton. "I'm taking him home. You should check on Davey."

Colton nodded and started back inside.

We left but we didn't go toward Heritage Oaks. Neither of us spoke as Lydia turned down a county road north of town and into a cul de sac for a subdivision that was under construction. Sitting there I could see my reflection in the window of the car, but only one eye was visible and the image was blurred. Lydia came around and tapped on the window.

"Let's go champ. Time to get out and move on." She pulled on the door handle. "It's never any fun beating up an old friend, but there are worse things and bigger disappointments in this world." She leaned in the car and kissed my cheek. "The night is young. Let's sit and admire the stars, Billy." She laughed. "Or should I call you Sugar Ray?"

Lydia and I didn't have sex that night. I was a virgin at the time and stayed that way until one drunken afternoon my freshman year of college, but that night, Lydia and I kissed, and we lay on a blanket she kept in the car for emergencies. Her body felt as good as I imagined it might, and she didn't have to spend much time touching me before I released a summer's worth of dreams and desires. My mouth wasn't the only thing that had a mind of its own back then. I'm not sure how far we would have gone that night if I could have held out longer, but I know she took me further than I deserved.

On the way home, I told Lydia I loved her. She smiled and when we got back to Heritage Oaks, she kissed me lightly on the lips. As I got out of the car, I noticed something in her eyes I hadn't seen before.

The next morning around 10:30, I went outside looking for Colton, hoping things would look better in the morning light. My hand was sore and a little swollen, a painful reminder of the night before. Colton was leaning against his truck and as I headed that direction, I saw Mr. Henderson carrying a mop and some cleaning stuff inside Lydia's trailer. There were two large plastic bags on the steps.

"Mr. Henderson." When I spoke he stopped on his way up the steps. "What's going on?"

"Billy. Good morning." Mr. Henderson started walking again. "It appears the Stevens family has moved on. Good riddance I say. They drove off this morning, early. I saw them packing some bags at about 5:00 and walked over to inquire."

I followed him in, and he set the bucket down on the kitchen floor.

"Mrs. Stevens apologized for not paying the rent or cleaning up. Said the mister had a new job offer in Texarkana, which I doubt. An hour later they were gone. I wish they had taken that trash with them."

As I walked out, I looked at the bags, hoping for a clue, some sense about why Lydia left.

"Hey, Billy." Colton called me over to his truck. "I saw her this morning about two when I got back from that party. There was some piece of shit truck in the driveway loaded up with boxes." Colton handed me a note. "She asked me to give you this." He looked at the trailer and then back at me. "Man. It sucks. She was cool." He patted my shoulder and went inside.

Walking back down the street, I opened the envelope: "Billy. This is it for me. The counselor at school told me I had enough credits to graduate so I filled out the paperwork without telling anyone. I wanted to tell you last night, but you decided to defend my honor instead. Thanks for that. My parents are riding in the truck while I drive the car. First chance, I'm turning the other way. It's time to bust out and make a break. I'll miss you and I'm sorry, but I have to find something more than what I've got. This isn't how I wanted to say goodbye, but I hope you'll remember some of the fun times we had. I know I'll think of you in the quiet and in the crowd. You made Heritage Oaks livable. I love you, Lydia."

And that was it.

Christmas was pretty awful that year but broken hearts heal. I had a few other girlfriends in high school and college but nothing serious until my second year of graduate school. My fiancée will be stopping by later this afternoon so we can pick out wedding invitations. My parents are going to drive in from Florida for the wedding. They'll stop by Heritage Oaks to catch up with old friends on their way back home and let anyone who wants to know that I'm married and doing fine, but I told Denise we won't need many seats on the groom's side of the church. They kept in touch with more people from back then than I ever did.

I sat, years later, staring out the window, wondering where Colton was and if he knew about Davey. He went off to A&M to play football, but he blew his knee out as a junior and moved to Atlanta after he graduated. Last time we talked, he was a financial consultant, but our conversations got shorter and shorter as the years passed.

It's been a long time since I've been in a fight and felt the crunch of flesh and bone. The most painful scars are almost never visible, and we can't ever wipe another man's blood off in the grass either. Some memories we hold on to and some won't go away even if we wanted.

The day before I left for college, Mr. Henderson stopped by the house and handed me a five hundred dollar check. He had stopped at Colton's place with the same for him, and he told me he was proud of us and our parents for working so hard at raising us right. "It's a too bad we can't clean out our past like we clean a trailer. Put all our problems in a big green bag and let the garbage men haul it away. Damn shame."

Lydia's note was on the table sitting next to Davey's fifteen minutes of fame. Mr. Henderson was right to be proud of my parents. They made sure I moved out of Heritage Oaks as soon as I could, but no matter how carefully we clean or how fast we move, there's always a little dust in the corner or something we miss in the back of the closet. Some things we pack in a hurry and forget about until a memory leaks through. But not all of these intrusions from the past are unfortunate, and I put Lydia's note back in my yearbook, glad I didn't read about her in the newspaper. In my mind, she's out there driving, twirling her hair with her finger, smiling with that sparkle of laughter in her eyes. If there's any justice in the world, when she stops for the night, someone will hold her and whisper stories in her ear while she leans back into his arms.

I smiled a little as I put the box back into the closet and sat back down, turning the page on Davey to see what else was going on in the world.

15

We Don't Buy School Shirts in This Family

Bobby Pritchard stood in the hall wearing a pair of faded, too-big shorts and a Wilkerson Wildcats t-shirt. It used to be his mommy's when she was in the first grade. Bobby is a Travis Tornado, but we don't buy school shirts in this family. She told Bobby she would keep her eyes open at some garage sales, but he knows she'll never find such a shirt.

Straddling the bedroom door frame, Bobby could see Mommy and Daddy sitting on the couch. He watched Daddy's head tilt back as he took a drink, and Bobby heard t.v. words he knew he shouldn't. Mommy's head was bent forward, hunched like she was trying to protect her head. Every once in awhile she shrugged the way Bobby did at school when he was tired. Occasionally he heard laughter followed by a grunt from the couch.

Bobby's daddy doesn't sound like they do on t.v. Not anymore. When they used to wrestle on the floor, Bobby could see his happiness before he heard it. Bobby would pretend to be a tickle monster, and Daddy's laugh would wrap itself around him like a giant bubble where nothing could hurt him. He hasn't been the tickle monster in a long time, and since last summer Daddy's laughter has become hard and short like the rat-a-tat-tat of a machine gun on t.v.

* * *

Bobby stayed home from school last week so he could help Mommy take lunch to Daddy at the steel mill. She called it a tailgate party, "like they have at those football games we watch," and she laughed while moving around the kitchen. Bobby watched her and felt the breeze blowing in the windows. The dry, cool air swept around him like Mommy's arms when she protected him from the monsters in his room at night. Bobby sat still as she hummed to a Patsy Cline song on the radio. "These old songs are the best," she said as the song ended. "We're going to take Daddy some fried chicken for lunch because this is a special day. Kind of like a birthday, only better."

Bobby, caught up in the excitement, put the salt and pepper in the flour, and he dipped the first four pieces of chicken in the batter. The flour and eggs made his fingers look like giant white worms, and Mommy pretended she was afraid when he wiggled them and made a scary face.

"They gave the job to Mike Tanner." Bobby's daddy stood behind the truck and started talking before he even said hello. "Tanner's that fat kid who's always got his nose stuck up Johnson's ass."

Mommy held a plate of food toward him. She didn't look up when Bobby slid closer to her but he felt her jump when Daddy slammed his hand down on the tailgate.

"That should be my fucking job. I work my goddamn ass off for what? I know this place inside and out." Daddy pointed back toward the mill with a chicken leg. "Tanner gives Johnson a blow job and all of a sudden he's runnin' the floor." He waved the chicken leg around like a miniature club.

Mommy held Bobby's hand, and he felt her body tighten with every word.

"That little prick might have a college degree, but he doesn't know jack shit about steel. Herb told me he got the temp wrong twice last week and damn near shut the place down."

Daddy raised the chicken, then pointed again. "We've all been covering his ass since he got here. Most qualified my ass. Looking to the future, Johnson says. What future. A future where that pencil dick fucks it all up." He threw the chicken down. "I've got to get back to work. Fuckin' dead end job."

Bobby and Mommy gathered the picnic things together, and they drove home while Bobby watched the houses pass slant-wise through his reflection in the window. He thought of all the people in them and wondered how many monsters lived in each one and who protected the little kids like him.

That night Bobby got in trouble when he spilled his milk at supper. He was using two hands like he was supposed to but his cup tipped anyway and the milk spread across the table. Daddy's "Goddamn it" was lost in the slap that knocked him off his chair, and Bobby watched the milk drip like little snowballs rolling off the edge and onto the floor. By the time the pain hit, the milk was puddled around him. He watched Daddy's wet, white footprints leave the kitchen before Mommy helped him up and held him in her lap. He fought against the tears because men don't cry like little girls in this house. Mommy tried to sing, but the words kept catching in her throat and her voice was lost in his throbbing ear as he tried his best to be a man.

The next morning at breakfast Mommy told him that Daddy was sorry for hitting him. "He just loses his temper sometimes," she told him as she rubbed her cheek.

Bobby saw dark circles under her eyes like she had drawn little smiles with a black marker. "When you go to work everyday, things don't always go all that good." She looked back at Bobby and reached to hug him. "But it will get better soon. And we'll have to be extra good for him from now on, won't we?" She brought him a plate. "I made pancakes just for you. Here's some syrup."

He watched as she poured, but he thought of the milk and his head started to hurt and he couldn't eat. As he left the table he heard Mommy start to call his name, but she stopped and he knew if he turned around she would have her head in her hands trying not to cry. Later, sitting in his closet, he asked God to help him be more careful at supper.

* * *

"Get your ass back in bed." Daddy was standing up and looking right at him.

Bobby jumped a little but he didn't move. It always started like this, but sometimes Daddy would change his mind if he stood still enough. If he was lucky, he would get to sit on Mommy's lap before she carried him back to bed.

"You don't have to talk to him like that, Jimmy." Mommy started to stand up. "I'm coming, Bobby."

"I'll talk to him any goddamn way I want. And you can stay right here until I'm finished with him." Daddy pushed her back to the couch like he was shoving trash into a can. "He comes out here because you let him." Daddy took a long drink. "At the end of the day all I want is a drink and some peace and quiet. Every damn night he comes waltzing down the hall complainin' about monsters in his room." He reached to grab another can and when he did Mommy stood up. "What he needs is to do what I tell him or get the belt."

Mommy started to move away from the couch but he reached out to grab her arm.

"Maybe what everyone in this house needs is a little reminder about how things are supposed to work around here. I may not be in charge at work, but this is still my goddamn house and I'm the man around here. Maybe we all need to remember that."

He had one hand on Mommy's arm and turned to look at Bobby. "I thought I told you to get your ass back in bed. There's not a goddamn thing wrong with your room, but there's gonna be something wrong with you if I come around this couch."

Bobby shivered when he heard his voice and watched Daddy take a drink.

"Jimmy, he's scared is all." Mommy looked down the hall toward Bobby. "Let me go and I'll put him back in bed." She tried to twist her arm away, but it didn't come loose and Bobby thought of a cat he saw one time stuck in his grandpa's shrimping net.

He took a half step forward and froze.

"You stay right here Missy."

Bobby saw Mommy's face twist and her eyes squint.

"Don't be trying to walk away while I'm talking to you." He looked right at Bobby while he held on to Mommy. He pointed again and Bobby could see the can dent where Daddy held it with his thumb and fingers. "Boy, you go on and get in bed. I guaran-goddamn-tee you I'm a helluva lot scarier than anything in your bedroom." He put the can down and started to undo his belt with his free hand. Bobby saw Mommy start hitting Daddy's hand, and she opened her mouth to speak, but all he heard was

20

Daddy telling him "if you're not in that bed by the time I count to three, I'm gonna take the belt to you. You'll think twice before you get outta that bed again."

"Bobby, go on back to bed now, okay. Mommy and Daddy need to talk for a minute."

Bobby's legs wouldn't move. His eyes darted from Mommy's hand and back to the belt. Her voice sounded like it did when she was opening a jar or picking him up now that he was getting so big and strong.

"Bobby, honey, Mommy will be okay. Go on down to your room and I'll be there in a minute."

"I'll be there in a minute," Daddy said, in a high pitched voice that reminded him of the girls on the playground when they were being mean. "You better go on, boy. *Mommy* will be there when I'm finished with her."

Bobby stood still and quiet just like he did Saturday mornings when Daddy needed his rest.

"Now, goddamn it." Daddy raised the belt in Bobby's direction and made a quick lunge.

"No, Jimmy. He's going. Go Bobby. Get in bed and close your door."

Bobby ran to his room. At the door, he turned and saw Mommy grab Daddy's hand, and Bobby saw him turn toward her, and as he closed his door he could see the belt come down and the sound carried to him as he crawled under the covers.

"Don't you ever, ever, interrupt me when I'm takin' care him."

Bobby burrowed as deep as he could, but he could hear the belt. A grunt.

"Turn around. Bend over and get the whippin' he shoulda got."

Bobby tried to pull the pillow under the covers and over his head.

"Jimmy, no. I'm sorry, Jimmy. He's in bed now Jimmy."

He could hear Mommy crying but it wasn't the same as when she cried during the day.

"Let's sit back . . ."

Bobby heard something break and a thud that must have been the belt and a quieter cry.

Bobby tried to tell himself it was a grown up movie on t.v., and he put his hand over his ears, but the sound followed him.

"Not like this Jimmy. No. NO."

"I said bend over, god damn it. Let's have that little talk, bitch."

Bobby crawled out of the covers and carried his pillow to the closet. As he closed the door, he heard a muffled cry and then everything got quiet as he curled up in the dark corner and the darkness covered him.

Bobby woke up when Mommy opened the closet door. The room was dark, but not dark enough to make the memory go away.

"Bobby, what are you doing in here, honey?" Bobby blinked and saw his shoes as his dream faded and he jerked backward like he was trying to hide inside the wall. Mommy stood hunched over, and Bobby could see the pain on her face when she bent down to grab his hand. Her bottom lip was puffy.

"Shh. Shh. It's okay, now little man. Come crawl in bed and I'll lay down with you until you fall back to sleep."

Bobby shook his head and looked toward the door.

"I already checked the room for monsters. Even under the bed." She looked at the door. "Daddy..."

Bobby could see her take a deep breath when she turned toward his bed. "Well, let's get on back to sleep, okay."

Bobby's legs were stiff when he stood up and when he crawled on the bed, he could see Mommy wince as she tucked him in, trying not to cry. She sat on his bed while Bobby fell asleep, and Bobby thought of a guard watching over him but he knew she couldn't stop all the monsters anymore.

* * *

Bobby wakes up as his door shuts. Daddy's work boots move down the hall, and Bobby is glad he's not sleeping in the closet because in this house only dogs and weirdoes sleep on the floor. Last year, he would have run down to the kitchen to sit on Daddy's lap before he left for work, and Daddy would tell Mommy, "Bobby can go to work with me today. He's man enough to run the press." This morning Bobby lay there listening for the back door to close and the car to back down the driveway.

"Bobby's still asleep." Bobby hears Daddy say. "Why don't you take him up to the store so he can buy a new toy." Things got quiet in the kitchen so Daddy must have sat down or stopped moving. The kitchen would be safe soon. "I guess I was a little rough last night."

"Jimmy, you can't buy his forgiveness." Mommy's voice is much quieter and not very steady. "You scared him last night."

Bobby gets up and creeps over to the door.

"You scare him every night."

Bobby opens his bedroom door and does his best imitation of Batman sneaking up on the bad guys. He hopes Daddy doesn't need to come back down the hall.

"I don't know if I can live like this anymore, Jimmy. When you're home, Bobby creeps around, hiding in his room." Mommy's voice is getting louder. "It's not just Bobby, either. I'm scared of you, Jimmy. What you did last night..."

"Shit, Missy. I got a little wild, that's all. Tanner's riding my ass at work and I needed to blow off some steam."

"Blow off some steam. Jimmy, you hurt me, you beat me with a belt, you tore..."

"Oh shut up. Jesus." Bobby hears the chair scrape as Daddy stands up from the table. "Stop bustin' my balls and make my goddamn lunch so I can get to work."

Bobby kneels down and peeks around the corner, silent as a mouse he tells himself. Daddy is walking across the kitchen, and Bobby can see the wind blowing the curtains into the house like miniature ghosts, but he can't feel the breeze in the hallway.

"I'm not busting your balls, Jimmy. You hurt me last night. You can't—"

Bobby knows the slap is coming before Daddy's hand shoots out toward Mommy. You're not allowed to talk back to Daddy in this house. Mommy knows that, but she does it anyway and Bobby watches as she stumbles backward into the stove. She stands with both hands on the edge as if she is trying to push it away from her. The stove holds steady and she stands up straight. Daddy moves forward.

"I'll do whatever in the hell I want. Maybe you need another reminder about who's in charge around here?" Daddy pulls his belt out. "Do you want to turn around or am I gonna have to make you?"

Bobby steps into the kitchen. "Stop hitting her."

23

Daddy stops and Bobby sees Mommy look at him. Her right hand rises to her mouth and then reaches out toward Bobby.

"Bobby..."

Daddy looks over his shoulder at Bobby as the back of his hand hits Mommy across the mouth.

Daddy smiles and starts turning, belt held at his waist, as Bobby screams again for him to stop. He takes a step into the kitchen and he sees the skillet in Mommy's hands. When Daddy starts to raise the belt, Mommy swings and Bobby feels rain drops as Daddy crumples and hits the floor in stages like a building blown up on t.v. Bobby watches red ooze out from under Daddy's head and onto the floor like dark maple syrup, the ragged edges of the puddle speckled with the dirt on the kitchen floor.

When Mommy drops the skillet, Daddy's eyes stare across the floor at Bobby's bare feet.

Bobby doesn't look up until Mommy touches his face with a wet rag, and he feels the breeze blow across his legs. Bobby looks at Mommy's face and sees tiny red drops across her cheek like she's been splashed with paint.

"Bobby? Bobby honey?" She touches his hair the same way she does at night before he falls asleep. "Daddy's sleeping now, okay? Oh, my god, baby. Look at me, Bobby." Bobby looks around her head at Daddy on the floor and then at her face.

The tears fall from the black rings under her eyes and the red runs into a light pink down her cheek. She kisses his forehead and pulls him close. "Everything's going to be okay. My brave little man." She whispers. "Let's go see grandma this morning, okay honey?" Mommy takes his hand and they walk toward the door. "She will be so happy to see you. We can get you some breakfast over there and I'll come back and check on Daddy."

Bobby Pritchard walks out the door in his faded, too big shorts and Wilkerson Wildcats t-shirt as Mommy wipes her face with the back of her hand. Through the open door, Bobby looks back toward Daddy and he sees Mommy's red footprints. The wind blows across his cheek, and Bobby squeezes his mommy's hand as the screen door slams.

In that moment he decides he doesn't need a Travis Tornados shirt. I'll probably outgrow it pretty soon anyway, he thinks.

It Will Get Better

"He's like a damn bobble head." Chance moved his head around in a kind of slow motion wiggle.

I glanced at him and then looked at the men in the parking lot. We leaned against a tree near the Glenn Middle School gym while my dad signed some papers, nodding his head when the sheriff's deputy or the tow truck driver asked a question. He rocked back on his heels moving his hands as he talked.

I could see my dad sigh as he shook hands with the deputy. He watched him walk back to his cruiser and then followed the tow truck driver to his vehicle. They said a word or two, and he stepped back, raising his hand in a small wave as the strobe lights went off. The darkness was stark and sudden, and we could hear the diesel engine clattering as the truck drove off with Chance's blue Mustang secured on the flatbed.

My dad took his glasses off, pinched his nose, and ran his hand from his hair line to his chin. He crooked his finger in our direction and gave it a little wag. We were already about halfway there.

"I'll tell you what..." he paused. "I realize two teenage boys have the brain power of a couple used tires, but you two," he shook his head, "I don't know. It's like you took a class in dip-shit 101. Right here near graduation and you're on the roof drinking beer and doing god knows what."

I hadn't been paying attention until he stopped talking, but when I looked up he was staring at me. He glanced at the roof and then at Chance. I followed his gaze, and I could see Chance's face in the pale street light, smiling as if he was waiting for my dad to tell a joke or say something important. My dad's mouth was partly open as if unsure what to say next.

I watched him staring at Chance for about five seconds before I closed my eyes, uncomfortable, maybe a little ashamed, and when I looked up he was eyeballing the roof again like he was working out some problem in his head. A car drove past. He folded his arms across his chest and watched the tail lights go out of sight. His shoulders slumped and I could see the disappointment in his eyes as he raised his hand to his mouth. He made a fist, blew on his hand and shook his head. "I hope drinking's all you were doing." He looked away, maybe lost in thoughts he didn't want to have. There wasn't anything I could say that would undo this moment for him. Or me.

"Chance, we'll drop you by your house on the way home." He turned to the truck. "The deputy had the dispatcher call your place but nobody answered. I told him we'd get you there."

Chance put his hand on my shoulder. I felt his breath on my neck as he leaned close and whispered, "Geez. A little dramatic, huh? It was just a couple of beers on the roof." Without looking, I could picture the half smile on his face and feel the heat from his hand radiating through my shirt. "Your old man needs to take a chill pill."

Just a couple of beers I told myself as we got in the truck.

* * *

Chance and I had been friends since the sixth grade when Mrs. Roach assigned an essay about our summer vacation. I wasn't in the mood to write anything. My parents were going through what my dad called a "rough patch."

"There's a lot of ill-timed things that have gone wrong all at once." He was sitting on the edge of my bed. "Your mother and I aren't really fighting. We just, well..." He closed his eyes and took a deep breath. "Sometimes people change and things get tough." He stood up, patting at my arm. "But we'll be okay."

I'm not sure either one of us believed him.

I'd already been in bed, right at the edge of sleep when I heard a crash from the kitchen. All summer I could tell something was wrong.

During the spring, my mom and dad came to my little league games together, but by All-Stars in June both cars were in the parking lot each game. They started working later and later each day. My dad went out on the weekends, and I would find him asleep on the couch, still in his clothes from the night before, stinking of cigarette smoke. Disheveled. He always got up when he heard me come in the room, and there was no idle conversation as he shuffled down the hall toward their room.

On the weekends, my mom busied herself cleaning or doing laundry. If my dad was inside, she worked in the yard work or found some way to be in a different room. She started visiting friends or her family more often and going to the mall, putting little presents on my pillow when I was at school. If my dad wasn't around, she gave me hugs and asked about my day. We all lived together but they were parenting separately.

Most nights dinner was burgers, fried chicken, and other fast food meals that could limit our time at the table. They started buying macaroni and cheese, hot dogs, and food I could make myself, my mom said, so I could learn how to cook. My diet and their marriage fell apart in equal measure. I tried to lose myself in sports, *TJ Hooker*, and *Gilligan's Island* reruns, but we lived on edge each night. There was no laugh track in our living room.

That night my parents had already been arguing. Bills, food, chores: I sat wishing they had both worked late again. They were cleaning the kitchen when I went to my room. After the crash, I heard my mom yelling, and as I opened my door she stormed past. She turned, jabbing her finger at my dad.

"God damn you. Go on and leave me the hell alone. You should have thought about all of that before any of this." She threw her hands up, waving at the hallway around her. "The house. Our life. This is you. Not me. You used to be..." She looked up, her jaw clenched. "I never even wanted..." She saw me and started to lean toward me, and her shoulders sagged, hands to her mouth. Breathing deeply, fighting tears, she turned to her room, closing the door more gently than the moment deserved. I looked down the hall. There was glass on the floor near the table.

My dad was already walking toward me, trying to block my view and get me back into my room. His little talk that night didn't help me get to sleep any faster. I wasn't sure what my mom didn't want that night, but she kept not wanting it all summer long.

My parents declared a kind of uneasy truce after that fight, but the silence around me was, it seemed, a calm before a rising storm. At night in bed, I heard whispered, muffled arguments, my mother's voice tight, my father hesitant but insistent, each one living at slow burn. It wasn't a question of if but when the volcano would erupt again. Keeping me out of the middle was the one thing they agreed on. At least we all realized the domestic minefield was no place for a 12 year old.

It wasn't exactly fodder for an essay about summer vacation either.

The Monday the essay was due we had to read the papers in front of the class. I read mine early since we went in alphabetical order.

"Summer really flew by this year. My family didn't take any vacations but I did play a lot of sports and watch t.v. My favorite sport to play this summer was baseball." I looked up from my reading. Jimmy Long stared out the window. Eliza Blose drew pictures and Ricky Wallace picked his nose. Sometimes it's best to focus on the paper, I told myself. "I watched a lot of reruns of *Gilligan's Island*. I think it would be neat to live on an island with friends. My favorite character is the Professor."

My paper was dull, predictable, and about average for any sixth grade writer whose primary goal was to avoid embarrassing himself. There was no mention of my dad punching a hole in the wall one night or my mother spending Sunday morning picking broken glass from the living-room carpet.

I sat down, happy to be finished. After four or five more papers, Mrs. Roach called Chance to the front.

I knew Chance before the sixth grade. I spent recess playing soccer, football, or whatever sport we had a ball for. While I was running around, Chance, Mary Grace, and the popular kids would disappear into a clump of trees at the far corner of the playground. Rumor was they played various games, some of them involving kissing, games with a different kind of physical contact than the ones I played.

There were days when Chance stuck around during recess, though. He was the fastest boy in school, and in P.E. Coach Pendergrass always made him and Jordan Charles team captains. If Jordan picked first, he took me, but Chance always picked Baker McGown first. Baker wasn't an athlete. In fact, I'm not sure Baker even knew what sport we were playing most days. Already pretty chunky, he had a face full of acne by the fourth grade. He was the kind of kid who always stands on the edge of any group or right next to the punch bowl at school dances.

The first time Chance picked Baker, I thought Coach was going to swallow his whistle.

"What the hell, Henderson?" Pendergrass stared at Chance and then looked at the rest of us. "Are you trying to lose?"

"Aw, Coach. We'll win anyway." Chance put on a big smile. "He's okay. Better that he's on my team than standing in the way for the other guys."

About two weeks into the eighth grade, Baker moved to New Mexico. Over the summer, he had gone from being chunky to downright fat, and Brad Johnson told us at lunch that his parents were sending him to a private military academy out there.

"I think even his parents thought he was disgusting. I went over to his house one day, and we sat in the basement playing Atari and eating chips. Every time his mom asked him a question, he burped and ignored her." Brad shuddered a little at the memory. "I felt sorry for her." He looked at Chance. "Why'd you always pick that guy back in P.E.? What did Pendergrass say that one time? He's so fat every time he runs, the car alarms go off in the parking lot."

Chance shrugged. "I don't know. Sometimes it's nice to give people what they want. Guy won't ever get picked first in his life. For anything. Ever." We all laughed. "It didn't hurt anybody and it made him feel good. Plus, it was fun to piss Pendergrass off every once in a while."

When it was time to read his paper, Chance strutted to the front. Even at 12 and the sixth grade, he had a muscular frame, something that developed even more when we got to high school. At lunch one day, I overheard Mary Grace tell Gina Brice that Chance was easy on the eyes in his button flies. I watched him walk by my desk, and I could feel my face flush and my stomach fluttered. I saw a short piece of string hanging below his back left pocket, knowing I shouldn't notice something like that. I looked away, the flutters now a tingle and then a wave of fear, not entirely sure what I was feeling but sensing it wasn't right.

Chance got to the front and cleared his throat.

"What I Did Last Summer." Chance looked up, smiled, and cleared his throat. "By Chance Angle."

The class laughed, partly because Chance had a pretty goofy look on his face, but also because his last name was, or at least was before today, Henderson.

Mrs. Roach looked up and frowned. "Cha—"

He held up his hand and started reading. "I had a very educational summer. Mrs. Roach would be proud." He turned toward her and smiled. "I spent my summer learning about marriage," Chance looked at us, "and divorce." He winked at someone on the front row.

Mrs. Roach stood up as the class laughed again. This was back when dysfunctional families were an embarrassment, not an opportunity for a reality t.v. show.

"In June, I lived with my dad and learned that my mother was a crazy, money loving witch. In July, I lived with my mother and she officially changed her last name to Angle. I also learned that my dad's secretary takes more than dictation and she is, according to my mom, a gold-digging whore who—"

"Chance." Mrs. Roach was up and walking toward him. "Come with me." Hands on his back, she moved him to the door. "Everyone stay in your seats. I'll be right back."

* * *

Life at home didn't improve over the next few years, but my parents settled into a routine. Divorce, I guess, seemed too complicated at the time or not worth the effort, but at least the fighting stopped. I did my best to avoid them and stayed in my room as much as possible, willing to sacrifice watching t.v. to avoid the constant tension that dominated the house those years.

I also spent a good bit of time with Chance. In middle school, we both played football and basketball. After school, we would walk to his house to eat, shoot hoops, or watch t.v. A woman who used to be Chance's nanny still came by three days a week to cook, leaving casseroles and other food in the fridge. Once we got to high school, the nanny stopped coming and his mom left money on the table. She and his step-dad were almost never home, either working late or "fuckin' around," Chance said.

"My mom's kind of a bitch and my step dad's at the office or out of town all the time. They buy me cool shit and leave me alone so it's okay." His voice was tight. He gave a small back-handed wave, but you can't brush away parental indifference so easily.

"I'm not lying," he reached for the remote, "it might be nice if they were around every once in a while, but we're like strangers around here." He flipped through the channels. "My sister comes home from college for the holidays and we all split to different rooms."

We sat on the couch with our shoulders inches apart, and I could smell Polo and dried sweat. He was wearing a dark blue Izod shirt and his eyes glistened as he spoke. More than anything, I wanted to touch his shoulder and tell him it would be okay. I started to raise my arm as he leaned forward, dropping the remote on the couch.

"Fuck them." He looked at me and stood up. "You're more like family to me than they are. Let's get something to eat."

I moved my arm to my stomach and watched him walk out of the room, hoping the sound from the t.v. was louder than the beating of my heart.

* * *

As sophomores, we both stopped playing football to concentrate on basketball. We were both about 6-3, but while I was all hustle and energy, Chance was style and grace. He had a fluid jump shot and a confidence that made him play bigger than he was. During games, we were a team, a couple who worked together to achieve a goal.

We still headed over to his house most days after school, but at 16, his parents had given him the keys to one of their cars. Some days we hung around his house, but most of the time we cruised around town. Chance knew people who would buy us beer, cigarettes, anything we wanted. We kept things pretty low key on weekdays and during basketball season, but Chance was a good-looking guy with money, a car, and almost no adult supervision. He liked being around people so we didn't have to work hard to find a good time.

31

Every once in a while, Chance had a party at his house. Never anything big or elaborate, but it was an opportunity, he said, "to get fucked and fucked up." I played along but inevitably Chance disappeared with some girl leaving me on crowd patrol.

"My parents don't care what I do as long as none of their precious shit gets broken," he told me.

I was okay keeping everything safe for him.

At some point, my parents realized I was sliding down the wrong path and tried to come together, sharing at least some desire to see me finish high school. In many ways, I think my delinquency gave them neutral ground, and we started to have conversations about college, drugs, and making good choices.

In the late fall of my sophomore year, my dad and I were working outside one Saturday morning.

"Your mother and I are a little worried about Chance." Dad stopped raking leaves and looked at me. We weren't much for heart-to-heart talks in our family so neither of us quite knew how to act. I stood holding a bag half-filled with leaves.

"I know you guys have been friends a while, but he's a little on the wild side. Always has been." His voice faded as he finished the sentence. I noticed the years wearing on his face and wondered, not for the first time, why my parents were still together. The strain of marriage was showing heavy on both of them.

"Chance is alright. He doesn't do anything that bad." I squatted and scooped up more leaves, wondering how far this conversation might go. "You guys just don't know him or what he's like."

"The thing is, son," his voice gained enough strength to make me raise my head, "we think you should steer clear of him for a while." He was leaning on the rake with the sun behind him so I had to squint to see his face. "We know about his parties and having girls over. The drinking. We're worried you're going to do something stupid or get some girl pregnant. The boys' parents are never home. Your mother and I have been talking about this a while now."

I looked at him and then to the house. My mom was standing in the window watching us. He coughed and I turned back to face him.

"I like hanging out with Chance." My face flushed and I put one knee on the ground. One hand still held the bag and the other rested on my thigh. I could feel the muscle spasm through the work gloves. "I don't really like any of the, um" I kind of stammered and rolled my shoulders, "you know, uh... any of the girls that come over." I looked up, about to say more, feeling something shift inside, but when I saw my dad's expression, I stopped. As he put the rake down and headed for the house, I realized I was squeezing my thigh and I relaxed my hand.

"We'll finish this later," he told me as he walked off.

I let go of the bag and sat down, leaning against a pecan tree near the driveway. I doubted we would finish anything later, and I wasn't sure I had anything left to say to him anyway. At the door, he turned, shook his head, and I knew the conversation hadn't gone the way either of us wanted.

* * *

Heading into our junior year, I started going steady with Whitney Rollins. I didn't want a girlfriend, but my parents would make little comments, wondering if I was going out with any girls or with Chance again. They kept mentioning girls from church and the neighborhood, offering to pay for dinner and a movie. If they couldn't ban me from hanging out with Chance, their new strategy was to fill my time with other people. On top of all their efforts, I overheard Tommy Williams make some crack about Chance and me being a little too close in the locker room one day.

Whitney was one of the prettiest and smartest girls in school, but her burning desire was to get "the hell out of this podunk town" so she could live in a big city and attend culinary school. In the meantime, all these "creeps keep asking me out. God. Some days I feel like I'm in a bad John Hughes' movie but the cool, hunky guy won't ever show up and save me. Last week, Mrs. Schuelke told us these were the best years of our lives and half the class cheered. If this is as good as it gets, somebody needs to shoot me now."

We were in the library studying for a World History test.

"It's almost enough to make me wish I had a boyfriend. Nothing serious. I don't want to be in love, just off the market so people will stop telling me to live for now and that I'm wasting my life. Jesus. Being single in high school isn't the end of the world. Your best friend Chance is kind of a playboy, but he sees it too. I'll bet he leaves and doesn't come back."

I knew what she meant. As much as I was enjoying myself in school, I kind of hoped there was more to life, a time when we could all be ourselves without worrying about what other people thought. I told her I dreamed every once in a while that Chance and I got recruited by some out-of-state school so we could play basketball together in college, maybe live in the same dorm.

We didn't get a lot of studying done that afternoon, but before we left the library, she told me I was "easy to talk to. You're not like other guys. That's a compliment, by the way. You listen. Last week, I tried to talk to Lance Pavlak about our Chemistry test, but he spent the whole time looking down my shirt. At least you know my eyes aren't below my neckline."

Later that week, she stopped me in the hall and asked me out, "No strings attached. Just so people will leave us alone."

What the hell, I thought. Relationships have been built on weaker foundations.

We'd go to movies and dinner together, but for the most part we double dated with Chance and whatever girl he was going out with at the time. More often than not, we skipped going anywhere and headed to his house to drink a few beers or smoke a joint. Whitney and I would be left on the couch, watching MTV or having long, rambling conversations about anything. We would make out sometimes, but I never pushed and she never seemed to care. She told me early on that I wasn't "going to get laid so I hope you're okay hanging out. I won't tell anyone we're not knocking boots every Friday night, but there's no way I'm taking a chance on getting pregnant before I'm 25 and out of college."

One night, though, after raiding the liquor cabinet at Chance's house, we wound up in his sister's bedroom, unsure in many ways what to do next. We kissed and I touched her breasts, slid my hand down to touch her, trying to remember what I had seen people do in the movies. Her hips moved as I kissed her neck and put my lips on hers. I rose on one arm while I caressed her. Her eyes were closed as I moved my fingers, unsure what I was doing but trying my best, wondering how long this would take.

I looked away from her and noticed the posters on the wall: David Lee Roth, George Michael, and other big-haired rock stars from the late 80s were scattered throughout the room. Chance's sister had a few trophies on her shelves, some ribbons pinned to the wall, but as Whitney began moving a little quicker and she put her hand on my wrist, I noticed a photo of Chance and his sister at the beach last summer. He was holding a volleyball. Both of them were smiling. I felt Whitney slide her hand on top of mine, moving my fingers with hers, her hips and body pressing more and more urgently against our hands. I looked back at her face. She shuddered, gave a small gasp, and I felt her body relax.

I rolled over to my back, staring at the ceiling. She kissed my neck and slid her hand down between my legs, looking at me when she noticed I wasn't hard. I didn't meet her eyes, focusing on acting excited and interested as she moved down my body and took me in her mouth. I thought I was too tired or I too drunk, but I knew that wasn't all of it.

I turned my head to the side, hoping to think of an excuse, a reason to stop Whitney from wasting her time. Instead, I found myself looking at the photo on the nightstand. Their hair was slicked back as if they had been in the water. Her hand was on his shoulder and his smile drew attention to his hard-boned jaw line. His eyes were alive, eyebrows raised with a hint of that smirk I knew so well. It was a look he got when he was happy and joking around. Her other hand was reaching across his stomach, trying to knock the ball from his hands. They were athletes and the summer tan brought out the muscle tone on his arms and abs. I could feel myself harden and Whitney moved faster.

Afterwards, she put her head on my shoulder, and I saw her notice the photo. She looked at me and she had a small smile on her face as if she understood something complex or odd. My face flushed as I kissed her forehead, and I closed my eyes again, trying to keep the right image in my head.

* * *

It was two days before graduation when Chance and I got caught on the roof of Glenn Middle School. I was still dating Whitney, but we hadn't repeated our one time encounter and we both knew when school ended, so did we. My plan, at the time, was to head to Cisco Junior College to play basketball, but Chance was headed to Spain the Monday after graduation to spend time with his real dad. His mother was getting another divorce and in the last few months, she had gone from six years of "parental apathy to trying to micro-manage my life. I'm like a pawn in some weird game of chess she's playing with my dad and stepdad. I want to get the hell away from her."

His dad was giving him a tour of Europe as a graduation present and then he planned on coming back to college in the states.

"We'll see, though," he told me. "Maybe I'll stay over there. My dad thinks I can get into college in London. Other than you, there's not anything left for me around here."

We had already been drinking when we decided to get on the roof. When they built Glenn, they planted a bunch of oak trees. On the back side of the school, one of the trees has a limb that sits about three feet off the roof. Six feet or so off the ground, the oak forms a giant V and the limbs rise from that spot. If you can get to that V, it's easy to shimmy up the limb, drop onto the gym, and have a perfect view of town.

Chance and I had a twelve pack and a couple of joints when we dropped onto the roof that night. We sat back against the air conditioner unit, popped the top and looked at the stars.

"I can't believe it's almost over, man." Chance took a drink.

"I can't believe you aren't going to play basketball. You're twice the player I am. Didn't that coach at North Texas offer you a scholarship?"

He shrugged and took a drink. "You know how Whitney is always talking about getting out of here? Me, too. I played ball for something to do. Gave me a chance to hang out with the guys. Probably kept me from getting into more trouble. As far as I'm concerned, there's no guarantee of mediocrity in life like happiness in high school." He threw his can toward a pile of empties sitting in a circular depression near the wall.

"Two points. God, look at all those cans. Think about how many kids have been drinking up here." He opened another. "If I stay here, I'll be back on this roof next year, hell next weekend, stuck in a rut pointing out which of those cans are mine. Denton is too close."

I threw my can toward the pile. It bounced off and over the wall. "Shit."

"God damn, Dylan. No wonder Cisco's the only one who offered. I hope you can hit Whitney's hole better than that."

We kept drinking and talking. A couple more cans went over the roof, but we didn't notice or pay attention. We would either pick them up when we left or forget about them. Didn't matter much.

"Time for desert," Chance said as he pulled out a lighter and one of the joints. We could hear cars drive by, but the night was peaceful and quiet. Sitting on the roof next to Chance, our shoulders brushing against each other, I knew this was the end of something. We would party after graduation, but there weren't going to be many more times for us to be alone. I couldn't think of anyplace I'd rather be. Right there. Right then. With him.

We smoked down to the nub but neither of us had remembered a clip. I took the last pull and flicked the joint into the pile of cans. As I did, Chance stood up, stretched, and I got up to join him.

"Well, this is it buddy." Chance held out his hand in mock seriousness. We shook, and he pulled me to him. I put my hand on his back, holding him tighter than I meant to and breathed him in, holding on until his arms loosened. He stepped back and put his hands in his pockets.

Red and blue lights started reflecting off the metal on the air conditioner.

"On the roof. Come to the edge so I can see you."

"Hell and god damn," Chance said as we walked to the edge of the roof. An hour later, my dad was driving us home telling Chance he could pick up his car the next day at Clark's Tow Shop.

* * *

Graduation was a blur. Whitney was registered for summer classes at Columbia and flying to New York Sunday night. We said goodbye after graduation with promises to keep in touch. I didn't see Chance on Sunday, but I picked him up Monday morning at 8:00. His flight was at 11:00, and we were going to get breakfast at a little place downtown. After eating, we drove through town one last time and then over past the high school. We still got to the airport early. No one was around when I parked in the short term lot.

We sat there and I could hear the engine ticking as it cooled down and I saw Chance's hand more toward the door.

"Chance."

We'd been friends for so long but there were things I still wanted to say. He turned in his seat but I couldn't look at him.

"Chance. Listen. Before you go, there's some things I gotta to tell you. I wanted to the other night but..." I took a breath, and the silence hung between us.

He touched my shoulder. I looked at his hand and closed my eyes as I leaned my cheek against his fingers.

"Dylan." He spoke softly. "Dylan. Look at me."

I turned in my seat and we faced each other across the console. His eyes were a hazy blue. Kind and beautiful pools that I wanted to get lost in.

"Dude. I meant what I said on the roof. You're about the only thing worth remembering in this town. God. Every time my parents were driving me nuts, you were there for me." He moved his hand behind my neck.

I closed my eyes, knowing already that I didn't want him to keep talking.

"But, I can't, you know? I'm not the one." He paused and pulled me into an awkward hug across the console, his breath warm on my ear. "I know today hurts, but it'll get better. I promise."

He opened the door and grabbed his bag from the bed of the truck. I watched him walk to the terminal and then turned my face to the windshield, resting my head against the seat, letting the tears fall. All the years of watching, waiting, and I sat, eyes closed, seeing that little piece of string from the sixth grade, wondering how anyone could ever be the right one if he wasn't.

Love is not a Dirty Word

Five-thirty in the morning and San Angelo is crispy cool, with patches of ice on the rooftops. West Texas in the fall—what we lack in color we make up for in clear skies tinged with wood smoke from early morning fires. My wife and I are headed to Houston for her family's annual Thanksgiving celebration, and the car is packed with clothes and Christmas presents we'll deliver early. I've always insisted on at least one major holiday at home, even though I would prefer all of them. We've started alternating Christmas and Thanksgiving with maybe one extra trip to Houston each year. My wife has eight brothers and sisters and twenty-five nieces and nephews. The first Christmas we spent with her family, I pointed to the noise and mayhem and offered to buy everyone a pack of condoms as stocking stuffers.

"Good thing we don't have kids, or they'd have to ride strapped to the roof." I slide into the car.

She doesn't laugh—who would at 4:30 in the morning? I envision driving the sun up, Diana Krall in the cd player, and a hot cup of coffee.

"Will you be okay if I go to sleep?" She rubs the back of my neck.

"I will unless you keep that up." I'm accelerating onto Highway 67 toward Eden, sipping my coffee and grooving to "Popsicle Toes."

"Mom called last night. Fred and Julie won't be around, neither will Aunt Barbara's family. Maybe a stray cousin or two."

"That's a real shame. I'm not so lucky about the Jesus-freaks, am I?" I can almost hear Jennifer roll her eyes. I take a sip of coffee. "I sure hope Neal will be there. His conversation is always so stimulating."

"Neal has his flaws, but Sharon says he's a great father."

"Good father—better caveman." I grunt a few times as Jennifer lays her head on the pillow.

One year at Christmas, Neal pointed the mashed potato spoon my way and told me my biggest flaw was faith in shared decision making: "You'll learn. Women shouldn't have a vote. Children either." He had been drinking beer most of the afternoon and, evidently, eavesdropping on a conversation we were having about our summer vacation plans.

Neanderthal Neal, we called him, but I was beginning to agree with him. Dictatorship has its privileges. I feel like turning the car around and telling Jennifer she's welcome to go by herself.

She's asleep and I slip into that driving zone. Images flash through my mind as I see the dash board lights reflected on the windshield and think about David Lynch's *Lost Highway*, "On the road again," "drivin' all night/ got my hands on the wheel." I'm fairly certain I'm butchering the lyrics, but it doesn't matter. The cotton rows emerge from the darkness, framing the highway, and I slip Mellencamp into the player. Little pink houses, teenagers holding on to 16 as long as they can. This is the driving moment I wait for. It's like that brief period right after the first two drinks: I'm comfortably numb, yet strangely alive and alert.

When my wife wakes up, we've passed Llano and the air outside is warmer, more humid than at home. The cool front hasn't pushed this far east, and I envision a sticky weekend in Houston. I've lost that early morning buzz, Austin traffic looms, and there's not a mid-morning cd in the car. I have to keep turning the air conditioner on and off to compensate for the air outside.

"I need to use the restroom."

"The world is my toilet, but I think we might have a cup in here for you."

She ignores me. When I look at her, she has bed head and her mascara has started to smear.

"You're lookin' kind of Boris Karloffish there honey." I drive with my knee and hold my arms straight out. She's not amused.

"We'll be at Lake Buchanan soon. I might could use a rest stop my own self."

I slip in the Oakridge Boys Greatest Hits, but we don't sing along like we used to. I stare at the road, watching the stripes fly by and listen to Donnie Carr and the boys "Sail away on the wings of love into the night. Cast out our fortunes on the sea." The lyrics haven't changed but neither of us seems that willing to throw caution to the wind and trust our future to the fates anymore. As the song fades, I notice the dead deer on the shoulder and then see the dark spot in the road caught by the mid-morning light Thanksgiving Day. The bloody patch she left seems, somehow, a perfect symbol of the trip we're taking. Families rushing home at 70 miles an hour have ground the flesh and bones into the asphalt. I see various scenarios in that smeared blood and none of them end well.

At Lake Buchanan we stop at Lake Shore Gas/Bait/Tackle/Beer. The gas station isn't near the shore and the prices are higher than any place else along the way, but they have the cleanest bathrooms, my wife says, and I like to make jokes about drunken worms with gas. The owner, we found out the first time we ever made this trip, is a San Angelo native. Every time we pass through, he quizzes us about families we don't know yet and places we haven't been, but he's never disappointed with what we've not experienced. The last couple of times he's asked if we left the baby in the car. "Good looking couple like you will have pretty girls and handsome boys. Make up for all the ugly ones I keep seeing around here," he says with a smile.

When my wife emerges from the bathroom, she looks better, but I follow her eyes and she's watching a mother and daughter stroll down the candy aisle. The little girl looks like she's had more than her fair share of candy bars, though, and in my mind I'm wishing they would head for the fruit. Or an exercise bike.

"Why would any mother give her overweight 10 year old more candy? Doesn't she realize she has to keep clothing that tub o'child?"

"Spoken like a man with no children. She's probably been good and her mom wants to reward her. And keep her happy for the rest of the trip. The carrot works better than the stick."

"She looks like she ate both. Hell hath no fury like a fat kid denied chocolate." I see the sigh before I hear it.

She rises a shade in her seat and then reaches down for her makeup bag. "You know some families get along fine. It's not all bribes and dirty diapers."

41

"I dream at night of wiping a dirty ass that is not my own," I say as I pull back onto Highway 29. "Schlepping candy bars to my co-workers like Dan does each year. Worrying about braces, the flu, buying the right present. Nothing says the holidays like traveling with a screaming brat in the back seat." I can see her looking at me.

"Don't you think, sometimes, how much fun it might be to shop for a little boy at the holidays? His face would light up when he opened his first glove or football? Love is not a dirty word, you know." She pulls the visor down. "There's something pretty magical about getting together to eat and tell stories with your family. As annoying as my family can be, I wouldn't trade sitting and laughing with my sisters about the stupid stuff we used to do for anything." She opens the bag on her lap. "Don't you ever miss your family? I can't remember the last time you talked to your sister."

I'm glad when she turns back to the mirror and starts putting make-up on.

"It can't have been all bad."

The conversation went the wrong way fast. The last time I saw my parents alive was two months before our wedding. Jen and I were living together in Dallas. Rent prices were too high to take the moral high ground. My dad called and asked if we'd be around Saturday. When they showed up, it was easy to see something was different. I joked later that I hoped my mouth was shut after I shook his hand. Live with a drinker for 18 years and there's a smell. In my dad's case, Old Spice and Jack Daniels— a kind of sickly sweet scent that lingered long after he left a room. He usually started around lunch and kept slowly swallowing all day. On the weekends, he chased his coffee with a little Tennessee mash for a kind of liquid brunch. My mom, at least, had the decency to wait until after 5:00 most days. Someone had to be sober enough to cook, drive us kids around town, and attend parent/teacher night, I guess.

They were holding hands and my mom's eyes were bright and her skin was clear. Even so, something looked off as they walked up the stairs to our apartment. It wasn't until later, after the police photos and the morgue, that I realized she had makeup on for the first time in my memory.

My dad was a study, though. He had his hair slicked back. It was 2:00 and his eyes didn't have that swollen look drinkers get, and I noticed, for probably the first time in my life, that my dad was a handsome man with blue eyes.

When my sister and I divided the estate, we found some photos of them when they were first married. My sister's a baby: sitting in a playpen, playing in the water, lying on the floor, just being cute in general. My parents were smiling, happy, and as I looked at the photos I saw them as they might have been without me, without pressure, without booze. I put the photos in my sister's pile. The day they visited, they had reached back to that moment, or as close as they could get, one last time.

My wife is reading as we cross I-35 and head through Georgetown toward Taylor. This route keeps us out of the Austin traffic, and we get to see dark land cotton fields. Every time we drive on these roads, I wonder what went through my parents' minds the last time they drove. On the way home, they took Highway 19 through Palestine, headed toward Crockett and then on to Huntsville. I imagine them on a winding road like this, with little traffic, when my dad must have seen a liquor store.

At the funeral his AA sponsor showed up. "Two months on the wagon. It's a damn shame he couldn't hold out any longer. I'll tell you what, the last thing he needed was to leave town. Something must have happened on that trip." He looked out over my shoulder, avoiding my eyes. I nodded at the implied accusation.

The day he died, he fidgeted through lunch, not eating much, drinking sweet tea, and letting my mom carry the conversation. Afterwards, we sat outside on the apartment steps while she and Jen cleaned up. I could tell he wanted to talk, but I had no way to make it easier for him, so I watched and waited.

"Son, I guess I wanted to sit down and say a few words before you got married to that girl." He paused and motioned with his head in the general direction of the apartment. Elbows on his knees, he sat hunched forward, looking toward the lower steps, and he rubbed his hands together as if trying to wash grime away.

"Now, I know you've been on your own awhile and you ain't never needed much from me. I also know I coulda done a better job as your dad." He swallowed, not much of a pause, but enough of a break to allow me to disagree, to come to his defense if I wanted, but I had no help to offer.

When he started talking again, he sat up straight and ran his fingers through his hair. He looked toward me, sighed, and looked away again. "I can tell you that I tried. Your mother and me married pretty young. Your sister was already a year old when we met, but I didn't care. She was the spittin' image of your mother and I loved 'em both."

We both stared out into the parking lot.

"See that car over there. That green one. Bob Jacobson—remember Bob? You played ball with his youngest. Bob just bought one of those cars and it runs like shit. I told him: Ford stands for Found On Roadside Dead." He had a wry smile on his lips, and I just nodded. I assumed he was changing the subject. I've heard that part of the story before.

"Yeah, I remember Bob. Big guy. Works as a mechanic out on Busher Road."

"That's him. Good with a wrench." He shuffled a bit. "These damn concrete steps don't get any softer the longer you sit here do they?" He shifted his weight again. "Anyways, once we had you, I got nervous about makin' a livin'. Every time I turned around, some asshole in charge wanted me to do more. It's what I liked about getting' on out at the Ellis Unit." He stretched his legs and put his hands out as if directing traffic. "You just get those bastards on the yellow line and move 'em down." He cleared his throat and waved his hand as if shooing a fly. "Movin' ain't always good, though, is it?" His voice softened. "I've been thinking a lot about the child-hood you and your sister had . . . All that bouncin' around... And me seeing all those wasted losers at work day in and day out."

His voice faded, and I saw him lift his arm as if to take a drink before he grabbed his knee to massage it and look at me with those new eyes.

I think that I needed to say to him it was okay. Tell him moving wasn't the issue. Let him know I was glad he'd stopped drinking. But I didn't say anything. I'm not sure, even now, it was okay. Absolution looks so easy when they give it on t.v., but I was more curious than forgiving at the time.

"Anyway. Listen. You love that little woman as much as you can. Don't get lost in anything that might get in the way. It's a sad day when a man can't love his family like he wants." These last words came out in a rush as he stood and put a tentative hand on my shoulder. He offered an awkward pat but didn't seem able to touch me twice. This tenderness was unfamiliar, so foreign to our past. In mid-air, he closed his hand and slipped it into his pocket as if that was where it belonged the whole time.

He walked up the steps and into the apartment. I didn't even have time to get up before he and my mom met me on their way out the door. My mom stopped to hug me, and my dad shook my hand.

"Figured we'd get started. I think we're gonna head out east. I-45's always a mess. Everybody's in such a hurry it's hard to hear yourself think. Those back roads are easier to drive."

We got the phone call at 8:30 that night from the DPS. The sheriff down in Anderson County found their car flipped and upside down near Slocum. They didn't tell us until we got there they found an empty bottle near the car.

"Whiskey. It was thrown clear, but there wadn't much left in the bottle. Toxology report's pending," but we all knew the cause of death.

I can imagine the sheriff walking up to the car, to the stink of Old Spice and whiskey, whatever sympathy he had slipping away.

When they called, Jen and I were talking about the visit.

"He didn't really say anything. Same story about him and my mom getting married. He did offer this strange warning about loving you and not getting distracted. I guess he laid off the booze for a couple of hours and felt guilty."

"Maybe he was trying to apologize."

"Whatever. It doesn't matter now, does it? He was a shitty father when it counted. Being a good one now is beside the point." I started flipping through the channels, hoping the Mavericks were on t.v. How do you explain to your fiancée that your parents always loved the bottom of a bottle more than they loved you?

On the outskirts of Giddings, I catch a glimpse of my image in the rearview mirror and see myself as a child excited about the holidays. "When I was 7, I asked my parents for a race track at Christmas." I notice my wife looking at me before I realize I'd spoken. "Sorry. I was just thinking out loud."

She touches my shoulder. "Go ahead," she says and massages my shoulder softly.

"Anyway, we'd made these wish lists at school and I asked for this race track. It had two loops and ran on electricity. The cars worked kind of like trolley cars with the electricity coming through the bottom." I move my hand off the steering wheel toward the windshield as if I were pushing a car forward. "The charge sent the cars through the loops and back around the track." I make a loop with my hand but in my mind I see the commercial for the track: The father's leaning over two blond haired, freckled boys. The mother stands in the background with a smile on her face, but it was the father and the track I remember most. Everyone's smiling and he has one hand on each boy's shoulder guiding them. Everything looked happy, fresh, clean smelling—Old Spice without the alcohol.

I change lanes and check my mirrors. "We were on the school bus when I showed the list to my sister. She's what? four years older, about to start junior high and mean as only an older sister can be. When I told her it was my list for Santa, she grabbed the paper and turned to Diane Taylor, calling me a baby for believing in Santa. All the kids in the seats around me started in—fake crying, sucking their thumbs. Finally, the bus driver told us to all settle down." I shake my head remembering why my sister and I rarely speak to each other. "She leaned close and slapped the list into my chest and told me not to ask for the track because it would make dad mad. I gave the list to them anyway. I didn't really care or understand money and didn't have enough shame not to beg. I probably sounded like that fat girl back at the gas station." I blink a few times wishing I could hit the pause button or rewind.

"Two nights before Christmas I heard my parents arguing. Mostly, I heard my dad. He cussed Hot Wheels, me, the teacher for letting us make a list. 'Goddamn expensive shit. Don't they have anything better to do at that damn school that make a bunch of fuckin' lists. He'll break the damn thing Christmas day anyway.' I guess I knew even before I heard them arguing that I wasn't going to get that track. Santa or no Santa. But hearing that sealed the deal."

I reach for a kleenex. "In my mind, though, I remember agreeing with my dad. I mean, he's my fucking dad, right. I'm 7 and he hung the moon. It was too expensive. We don't have the money. Stupid Ms. Beacham." Trying to blink back the tears, I fumble for the cds, but Jennifer puts her hand on mine. We're near Carmine and the road is blurry enough I know I need to pull over. I stop in front of The Antique Emporium. Their sign offers me treasures from the olden days, but I can't think of anything from the past I want.

My wife's hand reminds me how much I love her. She squeezes softly.

"So. The morning of Christmas Eve I told my mom that I didn't want that race track anyway. I'm eating a bowl of cereal, trying to sound tough. The more I looked at the picture, the cheaper it looked, I tell her, echoing my dad's words from the night before, a cleaner version of them. I don't remember if my mom said anything. I'm putting my bowl in the sink, not five minutes after I had trashed race tracks everywhere, and my dad walks in." I let out this little laugh, and rub my eyes while I sigh.

"Anyway. He walks in. He's had the day off, so he's already had at least one drink. He's got his cup in one hand, in the other a big brown paper sack. Never looks at me and I guarantee he doesn't remember what he said the night before. This bag kinda klunks as he sets it down, and I can tell it's full of bottles—a cornucopia of booze to get him through the holidays. I'm seven and I know what whiskey bottles sound like when they hit the kitchen table." I shake my head again. "'Damn stuff gets more expensive every day,' he says."

I try to mimic my dad, but my voice cracks as I lean my head against the steering wheel. "When I think of having children I think of that moment." I take a deep breath, ready to get the story over with. "Anyway. I remember realizing something had just happened. When my dad came in, I wasn't even there to him. He put the bottles away and mixed another drink."

I stop talking, feeling that emptiness that always follows spontaneous confessionals. I grab Bon Jovi's *Slippery When Wet*, but it's all wrong and I put it down before it even makes it to the cd player. Jennifer doesn't say anything as I back the car out and pull onto 290.

"We were making pretty good time until my breakdown there. Sorry."

"You're nothing like your dad you know."

"Yeah. Hell, here it is 10:00 and I haven't even had my first drink. Think you could crawl back there in the trunk and get that bottle of whiskey for me?"

"I'm not letting you joke your way out this time. That story... That's not right. You know it and I know it. Just because your dad fell into a bottle and couldn't climb out doesn't mean you have to. Look, my mom is a slave to my dad, but that's not me. Can you imagine me getting an allowance from you? Aren't you the one who told me you can't blame your parents once you're over thirty?"

We turn down 1488 toward I-45. Her parents live north of Houston. We ride in silence the rest of the way. Another reason I love my wife: she knows when to stop talking. I dig the Billy Idol cd out to try and make myself happier. Singing with Billy usually works wonders, but today I turn the stereo off after the first song and listen to the road.

As we pull in the driveway, I see about ten kids. Some are running around and others are hanging from limbs in a magnolia tree. It's pandemonium. Across the yard, I also see my brother-in-law kneeling down and leaning over Katy, his three year-old daughter, pointing to something on the ground. He turns to watch us drive in, and as I stop the car, he waves and picks up a pine needle. His daughter is squatting, pants low to the ground, arms resting across her legs, completely absorbed in what she sees on the ground. When he tickles her with the pine needle, they laugh, and in that moment I hear Jennifer's laughter.

"If my brother-in-law, that gluttonous neanderthal can love children, so can you." She opens her car door and we meet her family in front of the car.

I look at my wife's family, creating memories that crowd out the past no one wants anymore, and I hear Jennifer laughing, listening to her nieces and nephews talk about school projects, Santa Claus, anything and everything they can think of. I shake my in-laws' hands, pat a few shoulders, tousle some hair, and I smile at Jennifer when she looks at me. I pick Katy up and give her a kiss on the forehead. She hugs my neck, and I tell my wife I'll be in later, after Katy shows me what she was looking at with her dad.

Girls Are Nothing But Trouble

I didn't want to kiss Maria Williamson, and I sure as heck didn't want to dance with her. Maria's this girl I've known for a long time but she changed over the summer. I mean, not in a bad way or anything, but she started brushing her hair more often and sometimes I can't remember what I wanted to tell her. We used to sit around and talk about sports and teachers and stuff, but when I see her now, I get three times stupid and stuck on dumb. That's what my dad says when I get tongue tied around him so I guess it makes sense with Maria, too.

The truth is that life was a whole lot simpler before the sixth grade and school dances. Some days I wish I was still a first grader like my brother Robbie. He's kind of a baby and all, but what does he have to worry about? I mean, sure, my mom bugs him about brushing his teeth and she still helps him in the bathtub, but he never gets in trouble. The only thing he ever has to care about is whether he'll have enough time at recess to hang upside down and turn his face purple. When he gets hurt, he crawls up in my mom's lap. Last week I cut my leg and my dad told me to walk it off and act like a man. I'm not even sure what that means, but I know no one's asked me to sit in their lap lately. My parents would never admit it, but I can tell they like him best.

Anyways, there's a dance coming up in a couple of days, and it's supposed to be this big deal. Back at the beginning of school, Coach Dearborn told us she was going to teach us how to dance so we wouldn't look like a bunch of worms in a frying pan. Billy Burnett wondered how she knew what frying worms looked like, but no one said anything out loud

49

during class. She's what my dad calls a "tough old broad." My mom rolls her eyes when he says things like that, but she smiles just the same.

Billy said he thought she was more like a "tough old b****" rhymes with witch, but he was mad because she told him he had done-lap disease. You know, when your belly has done lapped over your belt. Billy's okay, and I like him and all, but he is a little on the chunky side if you know what I mean. I don't know how he couldn't be. Billy and I live next door to each other, about five blocks from school, but he won't ever walk.

He told me one morning he flat out refused to get up from the table if his mom wouldn't drive him to school. She told him that he could stay home and skip school, but he would never get a good job. When he said "Cool. When's lunch?" she grabbed her car keys and headed for the door.

Billy told me this story while he was eating one of those Fudge Rounds. Not one like my mom sends in my lunch, though. Billy had the one that's about as big as a frisbee. It's more like a fudge disk, if you know what I mean. He had crumbs on his belly and stuff. I'm surprised Coach didn't call him a fat slob. I guess being a tough old broad doesn't mean she can say anything she wants.

Coach Dearborn's okay, though. She's not as bad as Coach Brown back in the second grade. The story I heard was that Coach Brown played in the NFL for a year before he got hurt or something. Whatever. All I know is that guy was mean as a snake. He was the kind of coach who would make us run at the beginning of P.E. so we could "get loose." I guess that's not all bad, but Cody Moore once asked how long we would run and Coach said "Until I get tired of watching you or until someone pukes."

About once a week, we never got loose enough to stop running and spent the entire time circling the track. No one ever threw up, but Jesse Munoz did lie down one day in protest. It didn't work real well because he plopped right into an ant bed. When he got up, he ran around like crazy until he stopped and dropped his pants. I'm glad he was wearing underwear.

One day during P.E. in the second grade, Coach Brown asked Joey Peterson if he had poop for brains after Joey ran to third base instead of first in a game of kickball. Actually, he didn't say poop, but you get the idea.

So, anyway, Joey walked around the rest of the day sticking his head up to people's faces asking if his hair was stinky. When they said no, he would yell, "Yes it does because I have poop for brains." Except, he didn't say poop either. He would start dancing around, shaking his head back and forth like he had water in his ear screaming, "The poop is stuck. The poop is stuck." Then he would put his ear to the ground and grunt real loud like he was constipated. After a second he would stand up and start dancing around again asking if his hair smelled. Of course, he never used the word poop, but I don't want to get in trouble by telling you the whole truth.

We all laughed but when Mrs. Rice asked him later that day what the capital of Texas was and he said "I can't answer because I have poop for brains," except he didn't say poop, it stopped being funny. Well, actually it didn't, but I felt sorry for Joey since he got sent to the Principal's office.

That's when Coach Dearborn got hired.

Back in September when school started things were okay. We still played kickball and this real cool game with a beach ball and a plastic bat. Some days Coach would bring a football and tell us to divide up and play. Every once in a while, she would disappear into her office. Billy thought she was smoking cigarettes. Cody wondered if she had a boyfriend. What kind of person even thinks about something like that? Do you like to think about your teachers holding hands or kissing someone?

But I didn't care why she went to her office. Football beat the heck out of throwing flags in the air and trying to catch them. Talk about sissy stuff. In November, though, Coach was true to her word. and we started learning how to "properly conduct ourselves on the dance floor."

My little brother got to play basketball, and there I was listening to some old guy named Bing Cosby or Crosby or something like that. All I know is it wasn't any fun. I told you my little brother was lucky didn't I?

You don't even know the worst of it. At my school, by the sixth grade, boys and girls start taking P.E. at different times which is way cool. Let's face it, for the most part, girls don't belong on the football field. I don't mean all girls, of course. Maria is one of those girls who's pretty good. Heck, she's better than most of the boys. She's "fast as a cat" as my dad would say, and she's not real prissy about dirt and stuff. Plus, she's been the fastest runner in school since the fourth grade. And tough. Two years ago, she punched out Ricky Harper one afternoon.

Maria won the 60 yard dash in the fourth grade Olympics, and Coach Dearborn was handing Michael Taylor his silver ribbon. Ricky laughed and hollered out, "Dude, you got beat by a girl." Maria turned around and socked him right in the stomach. While he was lying on the ground, she bent over and yelled, "Dude, you got beat up by a girl."

Someone told me later that she was kind of sweet on Michael. I don't know about that but it was pretty funny watching Ricky squirm around. Talk about a worm in a frying pan. Coach Dearborn looked at Ricky and told him to "quit goofing off and get up."

My dad would have loved it.

But P.E. wasn't fun anymore. In November, they somehow messed with the class schedules and now the boys and girls all had P.E. at the same time. Every day we met in the gym so Coach Dearborn could play music from the dark ages and show us how to dance. I don't know how the girls felt, but I don't know any guys who were happy.

Well, that's not actually true. Melvin Alexander seemed to like it but he's the kind of kid who gets picked last for everything. Not that he seems to care. When we play football or basketball, he'll yell out "Pick me last. Pick me last." Once the game starts, he finds a spot, sits down, and reads until the game is over.

At the beginning of the year, Coach Dearborn would tell him to get up and participate. One day she made him play Frisbee football with us, but after he tripped about a thousand times and ran over little Philip Hernandez, she told him to stop.

"Good god, Alexander," she said, "you're a danger to yourself and others. I doubt if you can walk and chew gum at the same time. Go find someplace out of the way before you end up in the emergency room. At least bring a book tomorrow so you don't completely waste your time."

Melvin started listing P.E. as his favorite class because, he told people, "I get a lot of reading done. I'll probably make varsity in high school."

Like I said, he's kind of weird.

Melvin might be a geek with a capital G, but I have to admit I kind of like him. I don't go around announcing it, but he comes over sometimes with Maria and we play on the trampoline. I mean, I'm not ugly to him at school, but I don't know if I'd get in a fight or anything if someone was picking on him.

Don't tell anyone, but I'm kind of afraid of fighting. Last year, these two kids, Connor and Lance, started pushing each other in the hall. They were yelling back and forth when Lance reached out and hit Connor. It didn't look like he swung that hard, but Connor's lip exploded. Both guys got suspended for two days and when Connor came back his lip was all fat with this nasty scab on it. I'm not sure I could handle a fat lip or a black eye.

On the first day of dancing lessons, Melvin volunteered to "take a turn around the floor" with Coach Dearborn. "You have to learn the basics before I turn you loose with more modern music," Coach said. "This is Frank Sinatra, and I don't care what you think about him." She took Melvin's hand and showed him the proper way to begin. "He's better than any of the crap you kids listen to."

She and Melvin stood still as Coach started talking about counting and rhythm and steps. The girls stood on one side of the gym while the boys stood over by the bleachers. At one point, Jimmy Gavin starting inching toward the door. I don't know where he thought he was going to go. Where ever it was, he almost made it, but in the middle of talking about how important it was that the boys not step on the girl's toes, Coach blew her whistle loud enough that I almost peed my pants.

"Jimmy." Coach let go of Melvin's hands but he stood there like he was still dancing with someone. She looked at him and shook her head. "Jimmy. If you were just a little lighter on your feet, maybe you would've gotten away. Dancing might help you."

Jimmy was frozen at the door. He looked kind of like a squirrel stuck in the middle of the road. You know those squirrels that run back and forth in front of the car? Most of the time they make up their mind and dart to the curb before anything gross happens. Sometimes, especially if Billy's brother Frank is driving, they don't make it. He goes out of his way to run them over. One night last year he swerved to hit one and drove right up into Mrs. Swanson's yard and her pecan tree. Frank had a busted up eye and a cut on his forehead, but Billy said that he looked better than the squirrel. "Plus, he didn't actually get hurt running into the Swanson's tree," Billy told us. Mrs. Swanson wasn't all that mad about Frank driving into the yard; she had two grown boys who "raised a little heck themselves" my dad said. After Frank backed the car into the street, he walked up to Mrs. Swanson's house to talk to her.

She was standing there in her bathrobe holding her phone when Frank said, "Hey, Mrs. Swanson. Sorry about the mess." They both looked at the squirrel. "It don't look like he suffered much, at least. Kinda looks like he's doing the backstroke. Hey, did you know that squirrels always swim on their backs? Yep. They've got to keep their nuts dry."

Billy said that's when Mrs. Swanson started hitting Frank with her phone. She got him a couple of times before he even realized that she was swinging. She was pretty strong for an old lady. And fast, too. If he hadn't been a little quicker getting into his car, she might have done some real damage, Billy said.

My mom went by her house the next day and said there were tire tracks and a dead squirrel with Mrs. Swanson's phone lying there next to it. Bits and pieces of the phone were all over the yard.

"It looked like the squirrel had been talking on the phone when he got hit. Its little arms were stretched out with this grim, wicked smile on its face." She kind of shuddered as she opened the refrigerator to get the milk. My brother blurted out "Maybe he was trying to call the nuthouse." He started laughing like he was this great comedian. Typical of my mom, she laughed and gave him a hug. Later at dinner, she made him repeat it for my dad. I'm not saying it wasn't clever and all, but I think she overdid it a little. I mean, it wasn't that funny was it?

Anyway, Jimmy looked kind of like that squirrel must have looked as Frank's car was coming right at it. He shuffled back into line and the rest of us realized that escape was impossible.

Not that there was a line. Not on our side, at least. The girls were all standing and watching. For the most part, the guys looked like a "ragtag bunch of juvenile delinquents," Coach Dearborn said. We were bunched up, hands in our pockets, wishing we were anywhere but here. Guys would whisper to each other and talk tough. Matthew Vann stood there telling us he wouldn't mind getting "delinquent on Coach's a**" rhymes with gas. Do you ever notice how guys do that kind of thing? They stand around talking about beating people up and stuff, but they always whisper or stand so far away the people they're mad at can't hear them.

My dad says people like that have "diarrhea of the mouth." He always tells me that if I want to hit someone do it. "If you're not fully committed, keep your mouth shut and your hands to yourself." Of course, my dad also tells us every morning to "Keep your pants up and your lips to yourselves." I like my dad, but I don't understand him most of the time.

Last year we were at Pizza Hut eating supper one Friday night when Billy and Frank walked in. "That's a rag-tag bunch right there," my dad said.

My mom gave him a look and my dad acted all innocent. Talk about diarrhea of the mouth. My mom says my dad sometimes forgets that "little pitchers have big ears." She always points to Robbie and me when she says it.

My dad rolls his eyes and usually keeps talking. "Those two boys are going to have a tough row to hoe in this world." He looked at me. "Are you friends that younger one?" My dad could barely remember my name most days. He generally called us son 1 and son 2, depending on how mad he was. Or, at least, he acted like he couldn't remember anyone's name. Some days I don't think he's as dumb as he acts.

"Billy?" I asked him and looked over at Billy and Frank.

"No. I was curious if you hung out with Frank smoking cigarettes and drinking beer. Of course the younger one."

I shrugged my shoulders. My dad makes me nervous in public. My mom put her hand on his arm and whispered something in his ear. He looked at her and I could see him thinking.

"Those two boys are the spittin' image of their father. And that's not a good thing." He took a drink of his iced tea. "Just remember that you are what you eat, and you can never soar with the eagles if you're running around with the turkeys." He finished his pizza and looked at us. "Make sure your belly's full and your bladder's empty. We're about to head home."

Like I said. Sometimes dad's a pretty confusing guy.

"Pay attention. Boys. You in particular." Coach pointed her whistle right at Billy. I looked at him and he made a gun out of his finger and thumb when Coach turned her back. If he's the turkey, I wondered, who's the eagle in this class?

"You gentlemen will be leading these ladies around the dance floor."

There was some shuffling and I heard Farrell Church mutter "what ladies?"

Coach stared at him. "I expect good clean fun without groping and kissing."

Someone in the back said "That's just nasty," and I saw Billy make a weird kind of fist with his right hand and move it up and down in front of his, well, you know. My brother calls it his pee-pee so I hope you can figure out what I'm saying. Fred Lindahl shook his head and said "this is messed up."

Most of the rest of us stared at our shoes like they had betrayed us into walking over here today. I thought about how lucky my stupid brother was. He could still say anything he wanted because he was too young to know any better and P.E. didn't stink yet.

The music stopped. I looked up and saw Maria watching me. I hadn't ever noticed how long her hair was before.

"Time to partner up." Melvin walked back to the boy's side of the gym. "Boys and girls. Each group line up." Coach led Melvin to the edge of the basketball court. "Melvin, you stand here. Billy, you here." She motioned for Billy. "See how it's done gentleman. The rest of you follow suit." She clapped her hands and turned toward the girls. "You girls. Calinda. Start with you. Stand across from Melvin." Calinda moved down to the front of the line. "Claire. You next. Across from Billy."

I saw Coach look at Billy and smile.

This was a particular form of cruelty. Dancing was bad enough, but pairing Billy with Claire Burrows "Under Your Skin" crossed some un-spoken line. Let's just say that Coach Brown was never so mean. Every year since kindergarten, the teachers have put us in alphabetical order. Billy and Claire sit next to each other. Last year, on the first day of school, Billy told me "That girl needs to be taken out to the woods and abandoned."

We had heard his older brother say this the previous summer about some kittens that did, in fact, disappear soon after.

It might sound cruel to say the same thing about Claire, but you didn't have to sit in the same classroom with her. No one liked her. Not even the teachers. Claire had new clothes the first day of school each year, and she always had a list of the new things her parents bought her. One time she brought receipts for show and tell. Hand to God that's no lie. Mrs.

Harbin kept looking at Claire and then at her own clothes. She quit teaching about a month later and moved to Dallas.

I couldn't tell if I hated Claire because she was spoiled or because she was so snotty about it. I could've ignored that she was an only child and didn't have to fight with a little brother and that she got anything she wanted anytime she wanted if she wouldn't talk. The worst thing about Claire was her voice—high and squeaky like new shoes on a gym floor or a mouse caught in a cat's mouth. Or a tick burrowing under your skin. And Billy had to dance with her. Boy, if looks could kill, I'm thinking Coach and Claire would have been lying face down on the gym floor.

I don't know how the girls survived that first day. Coach walked around as we took little steps, making corrections here and there. I know I stepped on Julie Robinson's feet so many times she wouldn't talk to me for a week. No big loss, except that it wasn't my fault. I tried to dance, but every time she said ouch I would lose count. Most couples were floundering around like me and Julie, but Melvin and Calinda looked like they were actually dancing. After about five minutes, I noticed that Coach was leading couples off to the side, all of us but Melvin and Calinda.

I heard Billy say something under his breath, but I wasn't listening. I couldn't figure out how Melvin managed to avoid her feet, and Calinda looked like she was floating out there. But, as I stood there, I also felt pretty strange. I noticed while I was dancing how soft Julie's hand was, and I realized how nice she looked when she smiled. Of course, right then she was sitting on the bleachers holding her right foot with this pained look on her face. I did feel kind of bad and all, you know?

At the beginning, things went about like you'd expect when a bunch of 6th grade boys have to dance. With the exception of Melvin, most of looked about as "graceful as a hippo in a 100 yard dash," as my dad might say. All I can say is you didn't want to be a cockroach around there. Or a girl's foot. At one point, Farrell Church stepped down so hard, he broke Katy DuBois big toe. She was on crutches for two weeks. I'm still not sure if the old watermelon head did it on purpose or not. Farrell's this kid who's "so stupid it takes him two hours to watch *60 Minutes,*" Melvin says. He's kind of an animal so I wouldn't put it past him to stomp around while he's dancing.

Billy didn't make much progress either. After that first day with

Claire, he decided to pick his nose right as Coach told us to meet in the middle and choose our partners. He got the idea from Nate "the Nose" Bomgardner. This was a guy who in the first grade would get most of his right hand up one nostril and then pretend no one saw him as he wiped his finger under the desk. I swear you could see the booger buildup from the back of the room. Some days I felt sorry for the janitors.

Billy decided that if he picked his nose, none of the girls would hold his hand and he wouldn't have to dance. I don't think most of the girls wanted to be within ten feet of him anyway, but I didn't think he would pick his nose in class. When we started lining up on the third day, he got my attention by sticking his fat elbow into my arm and then he stuck his finger up his nose. When he pulled it out, there was this slimy, green booger hanging from his fingertip. I heard him say "Jackpot" and then he held his hand out toward Kelly Monahan and said "Your hand my fair lady" in this serious, gentlemanly way. Kelly started freaking out, yelling for Coach Dearborn.

"Burnett, what have you done now?" She stood in front of Billy looking at his finger. "Kelly, pipe down. Lord child. Be happy he didn't pick his butt." She turned to walk away. "Billy, go sit in the bleachers. I'd threaten to flunk you, but I doubt you'd care."

Billy just looked at Kelly and then stuck his finger in his mouth.

We all groaned and Carrie Nicholson told us later she threw up in her mouth a little. I don't know why Coach gave him the idea about picking his butt, though. She might regret that sooner or later.

Coach stood at the front of the gym near the CD player shaking her head. I've got to say that I wouldn't blame her if she snuck into her office to smoke every once in a while. She looked kind of like my dad when he gets home from work and tells my mom "Today was the kind of day that'll drive a man to drink." He always says this as he's pulling a beer out of the refrigerator.

I'm not sure if a cigarette has the same effect, but I can see how trying to teach Billy might drive someone to it. "The next boy who picks his nose in my gym will have to pick the nose of the person standing next to him. Now, partner up."

After that first day, I danced with all the girls at least once. At first, Coach would make us switch partners after about five minutes, mainly trying to avoid any more broken toes, but after a couple of days we danced with the same person the whole class. Some time in mid-November, Maria Williamson and I were sitting at lunch, complaining about dancing, wishing we were playing football instead. Like I said, Maria is what my mom calls a "tomboy." She almost always adds, "But she's cute as a button. Don't you think?"

I don't ever answer. Moms are weird that way, aren't they? Buttons aren't cute.

Maria and I have been friends since I found out she could burp the alphabet. It didn't hurt that she once farted while doing the morning announcements. I had finished reading the news and sports when Maria told the school we were going to have tacos, corn, and refried "beans, beans, the magical fruit, the more you eat the more you," and she moved the microphone behind her and provided the appropriate sound effects. When I told my parents what happened that night, my dad laughed until he cried. My mom shook her head, but I saw her smile just the same.

That day at lunch, Maria and I decided to be partners during P.E. from then on. Neither one of us liked dancing. Maria said most of the boys were either so stiff it was like dancing with a 2 x 4 or else they were trying to act all cool and smooth like MTV was there filming. Other than Melvin, of course. Billy started calling him twinkle toes, but I think he was jealous. I know I was. It was pretty impressive to see him glide around out there. I didn't think I would ever feel that way about someone like Melvin, but, well, you know, it would be cool to look a little less zombie-like as the music played.

"Last week, Rusty Grierson almost broke my fingers while he was holding my hand. God. He kept squeezing like he was trying to, I don't know, milk a cow or something." She ate some of her sandwich. "But Jonathon Schwartz is worse."

When she looked at me, I noticed her eyes were kind of green.

She smiled and leaned close. "That guy gives me the willies. He keeps trying to pull me close every time we dance. Carly told me that Friday he reached around and grabbed her butt and then asked if she wanted to be his girlfriend." Maria kind of shuddered.

I could feel her breath on my cheek as she talked.

"Does that to me and I'm going to hit him where the sun don't shine."

I got a little chill and felt goose bumps on my arms, but I don't think it was because of the story she told.

That afternoon, I offered Eric Grimes my tater tots for the next week if he let me cut in line to stand across from Maria. I'm not sure Coach Dearborn cared who we danced with anymore. She was so focused on keeping Billy and a few other "little miscreants" in line she left the rest of us alone. She was always using strange words when she talked about Billy.

Maria and I would start P.E. working on the dance steps like Coach taught us, but we ended up "horsing around" as my dad would say. It made P.E. bearable at least. Or it did until the day my brother ruined it.

Maria had come over after school. Melvin was there, too. He and Maria hung out more than I had noticed before. I'm not sure what they had in common. Anyway, Melvin, Maria, and another girl named Brianna from down the block were over, and we were all jumping on the trampoline.

My parents had hung a rope down from this big pecan tree limb right over the middle of the trampoline. We had this great game where one person would get on the rope and swing. The rest of us, that day my little brother was there too, would run around on the trampoline. The person on the rope would jump off and tackle someone. If they missed, they had to get back on the rope. If they knocked someone down, that person got on the rope. It wasn't the safest game, but it sure was fun.

Every once in a while, someone would get knocked off the trampoline, but my dad says "no blood, no foul." My mom refused to watch. She tells us "don't come crying to me if you break an arm." That's one of those stupid things parents say, isn't it? When I was younger and dumb like my brother, I used to imagine that I would have to sneak into my room with bones sticking out of my arm. Now that I'm older, I'm pretty sure my mom would help if one of us broke a bone. My dad's a different story. Sometimes I'm not sure about him.

So, it's like mid-November and the weather was nice outside. My mom wanted us to keep our hoodies on, but by now we were all down to t-shirts and my brother was on the rope swing. He jumped off to tackle Brianna and when he did, instead of grabbing her around the waist he wrapped his arms around her chest. I wasn't paying attention until I heard her say "don't grab me there."

My little brother didn't know what she was talking about, but Maria and Brianna started laughing and Brianna fixed her t-shirt. She got up on the rope and we kept playing, but I wondered why he couldn't grab her there before I noticed that Brianna and Maria had changed since last year. You know how without me saying, right? Up top and everything? Anyway, things weren't quite the same, but I tried not to think about it. I would've been able to if it weren't for my brother.

That night at supper, my mom asked if we had fun with the "girls over." She started to talk about how cute they are and how we used to "hate" playing with girls. She even did that quotation mark thing with her fingers when she said "hate." You know, all that annoying junk moms do when they think they're being clever. Except I don't want to say junk. I noticed she didn't ask about Melvin or mention him being "cute."

My dad was taking a drink of his beer when my stupid little brother blurts out "Why do Maria and Brianna have those bumps on their chest now?"

My face got all hot and my dad started to choke and laugh at the same time. A little trickle of beer came out his nose. I got very interested in my pork chop.

"Well." My mother started. She looked at him and then me. "Why do you ask, dear?"

"Shut up, stupid." I whispered out of the side of my mouth, but my dad reached out and popped me on the side of the head with one hand while he wiped his nose with his napkin. I wish our table was bigger.

"It's no fun to play with them on the trampoline anymore because they have these things, these little bumps," he held his hands in front of his shirt like he had two coconuts on his chest. He looked at my mother and pointed. "They're like yours only smaller and they bounce up and down when they jump." He moved his hands up and down. My dad shook his head back and forth with a smile. Some days I wish I had never been born.

"Well, dear as boys and girls get older their bodies..."

My dad recovered and he interrupted my mom, but he was looking straight at me.

"So, the tittie fairy visited Maria, huh?"

He can be a cruel man sometimes. I don't mean he beat us or anything. All in all, he's a great dad. He plays with us outside and he can be pretty funny. It's just that he's not someone who embarrasses easily, and his favorite saying is "quit your bellyachin' and suck it up. Whiners never win and winners never whine." It's not complicated but it's pretty different from what the counselors tell us at school. He always says that one day I'll appreciate his honesty. I have my doubts.

My stupid brother, of course, asked, "What's a tittie and why do fairies bring them? Is that like the tooth fairy's sister?"

I told you he was stupid.

My mother smiled at my father and rolled her eyes.

"I think we can use a different word than..." She looked at my father. He kept smiling and looking at me. "Your father meant to use the word breast."

I wanted to die. Right there.

"Maria is maturing and turning into a young woman."

My father looked at my mother and shook his head. He started to say something but my mother kept talking.

"Maria is still the same girl who likes football and the trampoline. Every one's body changes as they get older. Your brother's body will start changing soon, too."

"You mean the tittie fairy is going to visit him, too?"

Oh. My. God. He might be the most ignorant person on the planet. My dad laughed again. I thought he might fall out of his chair this time.

"No silly." This was right up my mom's alley. She kept going on, talking about hormones and genetics. I had kind of tuned her out until she said the word penis. Hearing your mother use the word penis at the dinner table will get your attention that's for darn sure. It's bad enough that my brother even mentioned that Maria and my mother both have, well, you know, things on their chests, but there ought to be a law about mother's talking about a boy's body parts.

Eventually, my mother stopped talking and my brother stopped asking questions. The rest of the evening, my dad would look at me and shake his head with a big smile on his face. That night I had this weird dream where I was dancing around the gym with Maria.

The next day during lunch, I kept looking at Maria when I didn't want to. She would talk to me about baseball or something, and I would be noticing her lips or her hair. Every once in a while I would look down at her t-shirt. And I would think about that dream. Stupid little brother.

The dance was getting close and Coach had started to bring in more modern "music, if you can call it that," she said. I'm not sure when the music was modern, but I guess it was better than Dean Martin. She kept playing these rock and country songs from the 1980s.

Do not ever tell your parents that you're dancing to George Strait at school. Have your parents ever danced around the living room? My parents moved the couch so they could dance last week. Of course, my brother joined right in.

If I thought the sight of them two-stepping was bad, it's because I hadn't even imagined what my dad would look like trying to dance and sing to Bon Jovi's "You Give Love a Bad Name." I'm sure he's talented at some things, but he sounds like two cats fighting in the alley when he sings. Have you ever noticed how your parents sing real loud to the oldies songs on the radio? It's like they can't hear their own voices. About the only thing more embarrassing is when they kiss in public.

My mom says dad had good rhythm when they first met, but I guess that goes away with age. I wondered out loud one night if maybe the bigger the belly, the less the rhythm. My brother laughed and my mom rolled her eyes. My dad grabbed me around the waist and tickled me, telling me to "dance you little smart mouth." We ended up on the floor wrestling until we all were laughing so hard I had to pee. That's the thing about my dad. I know I complain and all, but he's a lot fun most of the time.

I was glad Coach Dearborn never started singing during P.E. Every once in a while, I would see her mouthing the words to the songs, but I guess it's hard to harmonize with Hall and Oates when you have a whistle in your mouth.

So, last week we two-stepped and line danced during P.E. That was also when Farrell Church started talking about Maria. He never said it to me, but Billy told me he keeps talking about her chest and backside. He doesn't say chest or backside, but I don't want to sound like some fatheaded jerk and use the same words he does. The other day, Carol Daniels told me she overheard him tell Jonah Williams that I was pretty lucky since I was "getting some."

I'm not entirely sure what I'm supposed to be getting, but there's no way I'm asking anyone to explain it. All I know is that I'm definitely not in love with Maria because that's just gross, but I also know somebody needs to make Farrell the fathead shut up about it before Maria hears and gets her feelings hurt.

Heck, I didn't even want to see anyone kiss a girl when I watched t.v. It looks gross you know? Why would I want some girl's lips and her spit in my mouth? I kept wondering what Maria thought about the whole thing. I figured if anyone was going to fight Farrell, Maria would probably punch him out one day after P.E. Not that we talked about it or anything.

I would have been able to ignore the whole Maria thing if it hadn't been for my little brother. Last Tuesday, he asked me at supper "Are you in love with Maria? Is it because she has boobies?"

My dad looked at me and shook his head. "Do we have to talk about ti—," he glanced at my mother, "er, breasts every night?"

My mother turned to me with her eyebrows raised.

"Shut up you little fungus. I don't love anyone."

My dad reached across the table and hit me up side the head. "Don't tell your brother to shut up. What are you talking about, Robbie?"

I noticed he didn't slap him on the side of the head.

"Farrell Church came up to me on the playground after school and asked if Johnny was going to marry Maria. He started moving his hips back and forth like he was sticking his pee-pee into the swing set or something and then he started singing Johnny and Maria sitting in a tree, k-i-s-s-i-"

And that's when I hit Robbie up side the head.

That's also when I ended up in my room right after supper. He deserved it, though, and I would hit him again if I had a chance, I don't care what my dad says.

That was a couple of days ago and that night I had that dream again where Maria and I were dancing, except in the morning I was kind of disappointed that the dream ended when I woke up.

Don't tell Farrell, or anyone else, but I kind of like holding Maria's hand and standing close to her when we dance. It's not just that she's soft, but she smells different. Not bad different. Kind of a good different. And my stomach flutters a little sometimes when I think about her. I don't know.

Like I said before, life used to be a whole lot simpler.

I decided, though, that I had to kick Farrell Church's butt after school so he would stop talking about Maria and me kissing. Boy, my little brother is lucky to be in the first grade. Maybe my dad is right when he says girls are nothing but trouble.

My biggest problem was that I didn't know anything about fighting other than what I've seen at school or on t.v. I remembered that fight where Connor got a busted lip, but most fights are more like "monkeys slapping at each other," as my dad says. There's shoving and name calling, but I didn't want to do that. First off, I was pretty sure Farrell wasn't the kind of guy to stand around and talk. Second, every time kids get in a fight at school, they get suspended. My dad always said I could fight back if someone started beating me up, but if I started a fight I was going to get in big trouble at home.

But what in the world did I know about fighting? My brother is in the first grade and I might slap him upside the head every once in a while, but I didn't think that would make Farrell stop talking about me. Maria could help me, but I couldn't go ask her to beat up Farrell for me. God. If word got around that I asked a girl to fight for me that would be worse than kissing her. Melvin could help me tell some jokes and make fun of Farrell, but I wasn't interested in damaging his self-esteem. That left Billy.

Billy might be chunky and kind of lazy but having an older brother like Frank made him a lot tougher than me. He told me that he and Frank crashed through the living room wall fighting last spring. It's true, too. I went over there last summer and there was this big hole in the wall up about where their shoulders and head would be. It's kind of sad in a way, you know? I mean, I don't like my brother and all, but I wouldn't want to hit him so hard he broke through the wall.

"Well, the easiest and best way to fight someone bigger than you is to kick 'em in the balls." Billy was leaning against the wall waiting for his mother to pick him up. It was Wednesday. The dance was Friday. I needed to learn quick.

"That's like a cheap shot, man." I watched as Maria and Melvin walked down the street. More than anything I wanted to be walking with them, listening to Melvin tell some stupid joke. Standing next to Maria.

"Dude. Farrell is like twice your size. You aren't going to push him over or scare him by calling him names. He's likely to bust your nose if you try to slug it out." He leaned forward to look at me. "Are you sure you can even reach his nose? Man, I know his head looks like a watermelon, but that's because the rest of him is so big, too. I think the guy failed third grade four times. Joey told me he thinks Farrell's already shaving." He leaned back against the wall. "Remember last year when he hit Brian?"

"He didn't even mean to hit Brian."

"Does it matter? Brian's nose was just as broke. "

Billy was right. Brian McHale was the goofiest guy in school. Always had been. Back in the first grade, we used to go out to the playground at recess. Most of us would run around and play chase or climb all over the jungle gym. Brian would go under the slide and stand there staring out through the ladder rails. Every time a kid started climbing, he would start reaching through the bars and saying "You look yummy. I could eat you up."

It sounded like something my Aunts would say to my little brother when he was first born. They would hold him up near their faces, touching noses and making goofy sounds, talking like a baby. Brian used the same words, but he sounded like a "kid who rides the short bus to school" Billy told us at lunch one day.

It was worse if a girl started climbing the stairs in a skirt or a dress. He would yell "I see London, I see France, I see Janie's underpants." He always said Janie, even if the girl wasn't named Janie. Weird, huh? He did that until some girl actually named Janie kicked him in the mouth, "accidentally on purpose" she told us the next day. After that, the playground teacher banned him from the slides.

Brian never got normal either. On the first day of class last year, he announced, out of the clear blue, that he had "emotional issues." When we started laughing, he freaked out. He jumped up on the table in the middle of the room, pulled his pants down and yelled "This is what I think of you." He bent over at the waist and stuck his backside in the air and started hollering "I fart in your general direction. Repent you sinners." He kept going around in circles and saying that until he got dizzy or something and fell off the table. I was laughing so hard my side hurt. Billy was standing up yelling "Take it off." Ms. Keenum, a new teacher who looked like "she should be in the 5th grade not teaching it" my dad said, just stood there.

"I guess they don't have classes in 'Crazy Spit Kids Do' in the Teacher

Ed department. Poor woman." He didn't say spit, though. I told you he was strange sometime.

Anyway, after he fell Brian lay on the ground with his pants around his ankles until Mrs. McGee from next door came running in. I guess she heard all the commotion. She walked over and helped Brian pull his pants up and they walked out the door. Brian was gone for a couple of weeks.

When he got back, things seemed normal for a while, but then, sometime in mid-April, Farrell and TJ Walker got into an argument about something. Farrell was probably being a jerk, he's kind of good at that if you hadn't noticed, and TJ must have gotten sick of it. At recess one day, TJ walked up and shoved Farrell in the chest. Well, close to it. Farrell is the biggest kid in class and his head does look like a watermelon. Except he's got these two beaver teeth and brown hair also. Mainly, I think he's a fat head, but I've kept my distance. He gets in at least one fight a year. My dad says he's headed down the "wrong path" and my mother feels sorry for him, but they don't have to go to school with him. I just wish he would go down some other path. Soon. Before tomorrow afternoon when I needed to fight him.

So TJ shoved Farrell and Farrell stood there while TJ yelled "Blank You" and "I'm going to kick your butt" except he didn't say blank or butt. Billy's standing a few feet away and yells "Stop shoving each other and fight." Someone else hollered out to either TJ or Farrell, encouragement or egging him on. Either way. It's easy to like fighting when you're not about to get punched.

The rest of us were all standing around watching, wondering how long before either Farrell punched TJ or Coach Dearborn showed up to break them up. By now it was pretty clear that TJ wasn't going to run away. All I could think about was how stupid he was. Brian walked right into the middle of these two guys.

"Break it up boys. Violence is not the answer," Brian said. "Give peace a chance." He stuck his arms out with a hand on each chest. He looked like a "t" with his head hung down toward the ground. Actually, he looked like a doofus, but you get the idea.

The only problem was that Farrell had decided he'd had enough of TJ and anyone but Brian would have seen that his hand was already cocked and ready to punch. Even TJ was cringing and leaning his head back. Right about the moment that Brian walked in and touched Farrell's chest, Coach Dearborn blew her whistle. Brian looked toward her, and when he did his face turned right into Farrell's fist like he was waiting for those knuckles. Heck, as goofy as Brian is, he might have been.

Usually, people laugh at Brian, but things got quiet in a hurry when Farrell's fist met his nose. There was a dull kind of thud like when you clap your hands together wearing gloves. Brian dropped like a rock, crumpled may be a better way to put it, and blood sprayed out over some of the guys standing real close. The rest of us stood there until Billy said "Brutal."

Coach blew her whistle again and kids started to scatter.

"Church, Walker. You two idiots go the principal's office." She walked up and looked down at Brian. "Davis. You go get some paper towels."

I turned to go to the nearest bathroom.

"And hurry up about it. This boy is bleeding like a stuck pig."

As I took off jogging, I heard her say "The rest of you just go on. Except you Burnett. You probably started this somehow anyway."

By the time I got back, Brian was sitting up with his face to the sky. Coach was holding his neck and telling him to stop crying. "It's your own fault for getting involved." She took the paper towels. "What made you think it was a good idea to step in the middle of those two?" She handed him the towels. "I swear. Twelve year old boys are stupid enough to make you wonder why humans haven't gone extinct." She looked at me and Billy. "You two help our superhero down to the office so we can call his parents."

Standing there listening to Billy tell me how to fight, I pictured Brian's shirt from that day. It was soaked with this red stain down the middle to his stomach. His face looked like a bottle of ketchup had exploded, and Farrell hadn't gotten any smaller since last year.

Billy's mom pulled up at the curb and he started walking to the car. "Dude, you gotta do something. Fight him, kick him in the nuts, get your butt kicked. Something. If you don't, he'll keep talking. Either fight him or go kiss Maria." He opened the car door. "I'm telling you right now that kissing Maria might be the better choice." He sat down in the car and waved as his mom pulled away.

Thursday morning I moved slower than normal around the house. I thought about telling my mom that I felt sick, but I knew my dad would tell me to go to school anyway. Unless we've already thrown up, he tells us to "aim for someone we don't like" if we feel sick at school. He doesn't believe kids should miss school unless they are on "death's door. I pay taxes for a public babysitter to take care of you and try to help you learn something useful. Let's not waste any money." Mostly, he assumes we're lying about feeling bad and that we don't want to go to school.

I guess he's right sometimes, but I don't know, if I ever have kids I'm going to let them stay home every once in a while just for fun. Especially on days they might get killed by watermelon-headed crazy people like Farrell Church.

I wasn't being totally untrue about my stomach. It did hurt. Every time I thought about fighting Farrell, my stomach clenched together like someone was inside squeezing my guts. Most of that day went by in a haze until after P.E. Maria walked off toward her next class, but instead of walking with her and Melvin, I stood outside the building waiting for Farrell.

"Farrell." My legs were shaking. I once read about animals that have a fight or flight thing when danger is around. My legs definitely wanted flight. Farrell stopped. His head looked even bigger up close. "You need to stop talking about Maria."

Farrell looked at me and smiled. "Why? What're you going to do? Dance me to death?" He did one of those laughs and looked around to see if everyone else thought he was funny. He was huge and a moron. "Look, Davis. I don't care if you're sweet on Maria. I don't blame you, man. She's kind of a hottie. I know I wouldn't kick her out of bed."

"Listen, Farrell. You just need to shut up." Part of me wondered why Maria would be in anyone's bed to begin with. If she was, though, I was pretty sure it wouldn't be Farrell's. First of all, his head would take up all the space.

"Or what, Davis?" He started walking past me. As he did, he put his hand on my shoulder and kind of shoved. "Like I said, Maria's a babe. She's got..." He started saying things about Maria and her body that I can't repeat here but I'm sure you can guess. I'm not sure what he watches at night, but it's not rated G. Or PG for that matter.

"Look, you jerk, I don't care what you say about me, but you shut up about Maria." I said some other stuff, but I can't really tell you what I said because then I might really get in trouble. I will tell you, though, that it made Farrell stop in his tracks. God. Defending Maria's honor stunk. He turned, and I noticed there was no smile on that big old round pumpkin face of his.

"Davis. I don't care what you want to do with that little girlfriend of yours, but if you don't shut the heck up, I'm gonna knock you on your butt." No, he didn't say heck or butt. He has what my mom calls a foul mouth.

I felt like I was watching the whole thing from above. What do they call that? An out of body experience. I could see people starting to gather around and I saw Billy walking over.

"Farrell. Look. I don't want to fight with you," because you'll probably kill me, I thought, "but you can't say those things about Maria."

Farrell didn't say anything. I didn't get the sense that he was worried or scared I might beat him up. I could feel the sweat running down my sides.

"Davis. I'll tell you one more time to get away from me before I bust you in the mouth so hard you poop your teeth for a week." He didn't say poop, and I didn't want to debate the finer points of digestion. I don't picture Farrell as someone all that interested in human anatomy. In fact, he probably couldn't spell anatomy. Or human for that matter. No matter how badly I wanted flight over fight, I knew I couldn't back down now. I hate to admit it, but my dad was right again. If you're not fully committed, fighting isn't worth it. Maybe I wouldn't have to go to the dance after Farrell beat the snot out of me.

"Church, why don't you shut the heck up." I was shaken out of my thoughts of dismemberment by the sound of Billy's voice. He didn't say heck, and I won't tell you what the word rhymed with, but it got everyone's attention. I noticed he was standing next to me.

"Let's face it melon head, you're just jealous because Davis here might actually have a chance to kiss some one other than his sister."

I wasn't quite sure what was going on, but I heard people laugh and I saw Farrell turn and face Billy.

"Why don't you take your dumb, watermelon head to class and stop talking about Johnny and Maria from now on." Billy didn't yell like most guys do when they're getting ready to fight. In fact, he almost sounded bored. Farrell told him to mind his own business. He used different words and all, but Billy walked over to him while Farrell was talking and kicked him right in the nuts. Hard. Every guy there cringed and Farrell fell like a tree. Billy hit him in the mouth as he was falling and then kneeled down by Farrell's head. I saw him whisper something in Farrell's ear. I didn't hear what he said, but I saw Farrell nod ever so slightly.

Billy left right as Coach showed up. She looked down at Farrell and watched Billy go down the sidewalk. Coach stared at me for a few seconds and started so speak. Instead, she shook her head.

"Church. Get up off the ground and stop goofing off. I don't have time to fill out paper work because you're a screw up." She started walking to her office. "The rest of you go to class before I send all of you to detention."

I raced to catch up with Billy.

"Billy. Thanks man." He kept walking. "Why did you do that? Farrell is going to be pretty mad. What did you say to him?"

"I'm not worried about that guy. I made sure we had an understanding about some things, and I reminded him that my older brother knows where he lives." He stopped and looked at me. "Look, Johnny. You're not mean enough to fight guys like Farrell, and you've got too much going for you to kicked out of school." He started walking to class. "Don't start doing stupid things just because you can. People like Farrell aren't really worth your time."

Farrell went home early Thursday with an upset stomach, and he didn't say anything to me on Friday. In fact, it might have been my imagination, but he looked like he was avoiding me. I didn't care. I was so nervous about the dance that I didn't think about much else. Maria, Melvin, and I had already agreed to walk there together. Melvin did most of the talking, partly because I found it harder and harder to talk to Maria. I don't know why. She was still this close friend and all, but you know how it goes. It's like every time I went to talk to her about football or something, I was thinking about dancing and holding her hand. I spent most of Friday morning wishing Farrell had beaten me to a pulp.

Billy told me he wasn't going. Mindy Shaeffer's mom was supposed to be a chaperone, and he overheard her tell Jennifer Parker that they were going to have oatmeal cookies and kool aid.

"Man," Billy told me, "I don't want to dance and the refreshments stink. My parents have cable. Why would I want to eat bad food and watch a bunch of idiots jump around to crappy music?"

He missed out, I think, because the dance was actually pretty fun. Coach Dearborn was there with some man. Melvin said it was her brother because "no way does Dearborn have a boyfriend."

The DJ played a bunch of fast songs to start with. At first, most of the kids stayed in big groups, and, for the most part, we looked like a bunch of worms in a frying pan. Coach was probably pretty disappointed.

About halfway through the dance, the DJ started playing some slower songs also. When the slow music started, Coach Dearborn and her friend got out on the floor. She was good. It was weird seeing her out of those coach shorts, but it was downright freaky watching her look like a normal person. Melvin and Calinda danced also but about every other kid got off the dance floor like it was on fire. Maria leaned over and told me Melvin had been calling Calinda every night to talk. After the first slow song, the DJ played another fast song and the kids swarmed back onto the dance floor, Maria and I included. I noticed that my feet were getting kind of sore, and I was happy for a break when the music slowed down again. This time, though, Maria didn't rush off the dance floor. Instead, she reached out and grabbed my hand and before I could even think, we were dancing and I could feel her hand in mine as I counted my steps. We danced to every song the rest of the night.

Because we lived so close to the school and because the dance was over at 9:30, my dad told me I didn't have to wait for "mommy and daddy" to pick me up. "You're one step closer to being a real person," my dad said. "Don't blow it."

I think he was happy he wouldn't have to get off the couch and come get me. Maria, Melvin and I walked home together, passing Melvin's house first. He said he was going to go in and call "Calinda to make sure she got home okay."

Melvin lived about a block from Maria and after he went in, we walked toward her place. Without thinking, I reached down and took her hand, and she laced her fingers in mine. Neither of us looked at the other.

When we got to her door, she took her hand away and we turned to face each other. Life was pretty simple with a football around, but here, in her front yard, there were no footballs or coaches or races. It was just me and her and I noticed her green eyes and her pretty hair. I wasn't sure what to do or when life got so complicated.

"I had fun tonight, Johnny." She looked at me. "You're a pretty good dancer."

I know I was supposed to say something, but my brain sort of stuck on dumb again, as my dad might say.

"Yeah. My feet seemed to work pretty well. I'm glad I didn't look like a worm." God. Talk about a moronic thing to say. I tried a different tact. "So, do you want to come trampoline on the play tomorrow?" I just shook my head and Maria laughed. My face turned beet red. Why did Billy stop Farrell? I could be dead right now. It would be so much easier.

"I heard that you were going to fight Farrell Church yesterday because he was saying some things about me. Thanks." She had been avoiding my eyes, but when she looked directly at me, I could see her eyes sparkle. She lifted her face close to mine, and I closed my eyes as her lips touched mine. It was a quick and simple kiss and then she started walking to her door. She waved as she went in.

I sort of floated home, feeling all hyper and bouncy. You know what I mean? It's that feeling you get after making a great play or scoring real well on a test most people failed. My mom asked if I had fun, and I didn't even mind when she asked if I danced with any girls. Normally, questions like that are embarrassing, but tonight all I could think about was when the next dance would be and whether I should tell my dad girls might be worth all the trouble after all.

A Healthy Level of Sanity

Charles and his wife were in the art museum's foyer enjoying a glass of wine before viewing the new exhibit. He'd been on the road a good bit lately, and this was one of their first opportunities to talk without small children hanging on their legs. While Charles scanned the crowd looking for the wine server, his wife updated him about their two sons. Their oldest was perfectly content at home, but he would start kindergarten next year, and they worried about his social skills. They were discussing the merits of pre-school when his wife grabbed his shoulder and held her glass high to keep from spilling the wine.

He heard a soft "umph" and an "oh my" as he put his arm around her waist and pulled her close. Out of the corner of his eye, Charles saw another woman's knees buckle and as her glass fell, he grabbed her elbow. She already had one hand on his wife's shoulder, and her other rested on his forearm as she regained her balance. Charles could feel his wife's body against his side, but he also felt the heat of the other woman's skin through the sheer fabric of her blouse. His wife took half a step back, sliding her hand to his bicep as he put both hands in his pockets.

The other woman turned toward them. Her hair shimmered as she brushed a loose strand away from her face. Hazel eyes. Skin slightly freckled. A woman comfortable without makeup. She tucked her hair behind her ear and an earring caught the gallery lights. She had taste, "someone who knows how to dress without ostentation," his wife would say later. "I'll bet she comes from money."

"I am so sorry," she said as she put her hand on Charles' shoulder,

75

reaching down to adjust a silver pump. When she finished, she smoothed the ends of her blouse and moved as a waiter came over with a small mop. At first, he thought she might offer to help, but she simply apologized before looking back at them. There was a casual disregard for anyone else in the room as she spoke to them.

"Are you okay? My goodness. I've made a mess of your shoes," she said looking at Charles. "And the cuffs of your pants." She turned to his wife. "I hope I didn't spill anything on your lovely dress. That's a beautiful color for you."

His wife stepped away from him. She took a sip of wine as the woman opened her purse and pulled out a card.

"Here's my number." She handed Charles the card. "Joan Simmons. Art lover and resident klutz. I should practice walking in these shoes before going out in public."

He introduced himself and Suzie, his wife, who nodded and smiled but Charles could tell she didn't mean it—only one of them was happy to meet Joan. They were not going to say nice things about her later.

"Don't worry about it," he said. "We have small children. The wine will complement the apple juice and other stains."

Two weeks after the opening, he got his first email from Joan:

From: Joan Simmons <joan.simmons124@hotmail.com>
To: Charles William <charles.williams@yahoo.com>
Sent: Monday, September 10, 2003 8:45 AM
Subject: Forgive and Forget?

Dear Mr. William (Charles?),

Mea culpa! I hadn't heard from you yet, so I googled your name. If this isn't the Charles William I spilled wine on Friday night two weeks ago, please disregard.

If it is, you simply must let me reimburse you for anything I've ruined. They shouldn't serve food and drink, especially drink, to people in high heels. Please let me know how much it costs to clean your shoes, slacks, and your wife's dress so I can reimburse your expenses!

Hoping you will forgive but not forget,
Joan Simmons (resident klutz)

He was surprised to hear from her. After she walked away, they saw her periodically as they looked at the artwork. The exhibit, fifty-two sketches titled "Scenes from Stango's: Tuesdays at 8:00 a.m.," were hanging on the gallery walls. Every Tuesday morning for a year, the artist sat on the patio of a locally owned, downtown coffee shop and sketched. Hailed already by critics as "creating coherence out of the juxtaposition of urban loneliness and the quest for connectivity on the crowded sidewalks of America," the sketches featured "local faces ignoring the inevitable decay and detritus that infests most downtown areas offset by occasional acts of goodwill that offer a small measure of hope for humanity. These seemingly meaningless moments, frozen on the canvas and framed, remind us that each morning of our daily life has the potential to be memorable or mundane."

The collection created quite a stir and *Art in America* and the *New York Times* were on hand to review the opening: everyone else was there to see how many friends and neighbors they might recognize in each sketch. Joan was in four of them.

It was easy to see why. She was the kind of person who attracted people, engaged them in conversation, reached out and touched strangers. Both reserved in public, Charles and his wife envied people like her. They sat on the back row—at church, movie theaters, classrooms—so they could watch and later speculate about other people's lives.

They had, in fact, met in college at a required Business Symposium. Suzie was sitting in the back row, making sarcastic comments about the keynote speaker. Charles had eavesdropped and then joined in with a few snide remarks about the man's hair that revealed a shared cynicism about such events. They went out for coffee later that week and married after graduation.

When they were leaving the opening that night, they saw Joan across the room near the gift shop. She had one hand on the arm of a well-dressed man and an empty glass in the other. As Charles helped his wife with her coat, he watched Joan and imagined her in a sketch: "Complicated Woman." The image on canvas would not be angelic. It would show someone flawed but with grace and an intensity that glowed. She would be surrounded by people watching her while she focused on everyone and no one at the same time. Like the sketches they viewed that night, the picture would explore the complexity of relationships in crowded spaces, Charles thought. All those people standing near her, and she still looks so alone.

Life, though, isn't captured by the sketch artist's pen. When Joan set her glass down on a passing waiter's tray, she looked up and saw Charles watching her. With his wife's coat in his hand, he raised two fingers and nodded, "There's that woman, what's her name—Joan." His wife looked up as Joan turned back to the man.

"She found a date for the night. And here I was worried she might have to go home alone," she said with more sharpness than he expected.

"Maybe it's her husband." His wife looked at him and shook her head.

"I'll bet she's either divorced or never married. She's a beautiful woman who flirts without knowing that's what she's doing. Ms. Joan Simmons is every husband's dream and every wife's nightmare," she said matter-of-factly as they turned to go home.

When Charles received that first e-mail from Joan, he thought of his wife's statement at the gallery. They'd been married for eight years at the time. He worked in sales and made enough so that Suzie could quit her teaching job and stay home with their children. The most exciting thing to happen recently, other than the birth of their second son, was paying off her student loans two years early. They owed twenty-two more years on their house, three years on their second car, and they were considering buying the kids a dog for Christmas.

In those eight years, Charles had never had an affair and, truth be told, never really considered being unfaithful despite years on the road and lonely nights in hotel rooms. Whenever they would hear about friends who cheated on each other, Charles would reassure his wife, telling her that "Affairs are too much work. What's the point: divorce, broken hearts and homes for sex? I'm eternally faithful." It was his standard line, followed by a reassuring hug. "Unless Halle Berry shows up at the door naked. Then, all bets are off. I mean, I love you and everything, but she's pretty hot."

"And you're safe until the plumber shows up looking like George Clooney," she'd say when she was in a good mood.

He'd been true to that claim. No Halle Berry, no affair and evidently all their repairmen had been ugly. Charles wouldn't deny the occasional fantasy about the lonely waitress in some backwoods diner, and before their oldest son was born he and Suzie might role play such a meeting, but what works in the fantasy world doesn't apply to day to day life. Halle Berry doesn't do diners.

Their lives might not have the excitement and romance of a t.v. sitcom, but they'd settled into a routine that kept them satisfied. He knew what kind of movies she liked, she cooked his favorite foods, and they both knew where and when to touch each other. They had become comfortable together, and they tried to do the best they could. Most days that was enough.

Then he met Joan.

Reading her email, he could see her standing near a painting, auburn hair at mid-back. She wore black slacks and a green blouse with sheer sleeves. A darker, forest-green scarf covering her shoulders was pinned with a silver broach near her left shoulder. She tilted her head slightly when she looked at a painting but never when she talked to someone.

It took Charles at least thirty minutes to write a brief response. Every keystroke, he imagined, turned the inanimate image into a live action scene. This was no early morning sidewalk sketch.

From: Charles Williams <charles.williams@yahoo.com>
To: Joan Simmons <joan.simmons124@hotmail.com>
Sent: Monday, September 10, 2003 9:30 AM
Subject: All is forgiven

Joan:

Please call me Charles. Sorry to disappoint you, but I don't wear expensive enough clothes to dry clean, and my wife's dress was unharmed during the evening's excitement. Lucky me, huh?

I'll happily bill you for the time required to wipe and polish my shoes and the water necessary to wash the slacks at home, but other than that, you'll have to make up for the spill some other way.

I hope you enjoyed the opening.
Charles

He labored over the wording and the tone, trying to sound flirtatious without sounding forward, but it had been a long time since he had talked anything but business with a woman not his wife.

Opening his e-mail the next morning was like Valentine's Day in elementary school. Charles was nervous and excited, hoping the prettiest girl in class would put a card in his decorated shoebox but unsure what he would do if she did. When he saw that Joan had responded, he glanced around. No one was near, but he still shut the office door.

From: Joan Simmons <joan.simmons124@hotmail.com>
To: Charles Williams <charles.williams@yahoo.com>
Sent: Tuesday, September 13, 2003 8:15 AM
Subject: Re: All is forgiven

Charles,
Good morning! I was out of the office almost all day. Lawyers! They really do use legal pads and we were out. It was a true emergency! The fate of the free world and corporate tax breaks rested on my shoulders.

I enjoyed the opening. I sometimes wonder which moment of my life will be the most important and if we have to quest for connectivity or if it just happens?

Do you know the artist or are you a museum lover?

Make up for the spill, huh?
Joan

After he read her e-mail, Charles realized he was sitting on the edge of his seat. He read his other e-mails, deferring the gratification of writing back until his work was complete.

From: Charles Williams <charles.williams@yahoo.com>
To: Joan Simmons <joan.simmons124@hotmail.com>
Sent: Tuesday, September 13, 2003 10:30 AM
Subject: Re: All is forgiven

Joan,

I have some ideas but I can't share them, this being the company's computer and all.

We go to the museum periodically, but I travel a lot selling medical supplies to regional hospitals throughout west Texas. I know everything you ever wanted to know (and more) about catheters.

We also have small children. An exciting night out for us is eating at a restaurant without a playground. We spend most of our days trying to keep a healthy level of sanity with the connections we already have.

Charles

They began e-mailing every other day, sometimes three or four times a week. Charles always waited about 24 hours, choosing his words carefully, creating this other world that his family and friends knew nothing about. Talking to Joan reminded him of being single and on the make at the local bar near his college campus. Sometimes after he e-mailed Joan, he would think back to his early life with Suzie. At the time, before marriage, mortgages, and the grind of the every day, there was an urgency and sexual tension that was both exhilarating and exhausting. Every conversation seemed magical and full of possibilities. These were rare moments in their house now. School, bed times, dental appointments—the realities of daily life replaced the energy of youth. Comfortable was another word for dull these days.

With Joan, Charles felt like he could recapture some of that past. He would e-mail after a trip, telling Joan about hospital staffs, bands in small west Texas bars, wacky waitresses included. She wrote about lawsuits or inside law firm jokes. As Assistant Public Relations Director, she had to attend any social gathering of import in town, and she knew all the gossip. At times these parties excited her, she told Charles. Other times she recognized her job was to look pretty, "show some cleavage and pretend to care about old, rich men with potential legal problems. Flattering but exhausting," especially when her boss would suggest which of her blouses to wear. "Some days I can't tell if he's the Director of PR or a glorified, well-paid pimp. I guess we know what that makes me."

The cyber world offered them, Charles told himself, all the thrill and none of the dangers. He always avoided any conversations about meeting for coffee or a drink if Joan mentioned the possibility.

In March Joan took a two week vacation. She said she was going to "Dallas, Plano, and the world beyond." Without her e-mails, Charles tried to resurrect his wife's past playfulness. At night, after the kids were in bed, he flirted, made risqué jokes, tried to engage her in the kind of banter he and Joan shared on the computer. After a couple of days, she asked why he was acting so strange, wondering if he was "okay or if something's going on a work?"

"I'm just trying to liven things up around here," he told her in a voice angrier than the moment called for. They slept as far apart as the queen size bed allowed that night.

He also started dreaming of Joan. Some of the dreams were sexual, and he would see them in a motel room or on some non-descript beach alone at sunset. Each time, Charles would wake up hard and stiff. One night he had a wet dream, something he hadn't done since he was a teenager. When he came out of the bathroom after cleaning up, Suzie stirred, rolling over after a long day watching their boys, and Charles took his pillow to the couch, spending a restless, guilty night in the living room.

In late March, he had a different kind of dream. They were driving and talking, but Joan's voice faded away until he couldn't hear her anymore. Charles shouted to her, but her mouth kept moving with no sound, and then she opened the car door. He tried to reach out to her, but his hands were glued to the steering wheel and no matter how hard he yanked or struggled, his fingers wouldn't come free. Joan looked at him sadly and leaned into the dark void right as his hands came free of the wheel, and he lunged across the console. He jerked awake, breathing heavily. He lay there watching Suzie sleep, wondering how long it had been since he reached out for her early in the morning, wishing he didn't feel so empty inside.

When the e-mails from Joan should have resumed, they didn't. Charles wrote, asking if she was okay, playfully chiding her for forgetting him, but nothing came back. He wanted to call her office, look her name up in the phone book maybe and ring her house, "to make sure she was okay," he told himself. Eventually, he assumed she had moved on, and he found some measure of solace in being a beautiful woman's passing fancy. It was fun while it lasted, he thought, but she's young and single. There's no reason, he told himself, to expect her to keep in touch with a married man.

From: Joan Simmons <joan.simmons124@hotmail.com>
To: Charles Williams <charles.williams@yahoo.com>
Sent: Friday, May 17, 2004 4:41 PM
Subject: In sanity or out of it

Dear Charles,

I got your e-mail asking about my vacation. Yes I returned and yes I am safe.

I did return in one piece, but not with peace of mind. At the office, I'm more public relations than legal assistant, but we both know that PR in this town stands for "pretty rack" if you're a woman.

When I got back from my vacation, I saw you and your family at Enrique's downtown. You didn't see me, and I didn't know if I should come over and say hello or not.

Do you remember earlier this spring seeing each other at the baseball game? I introduced myself to your wife. She seemed surprised that I remembered her. And you. Everything that night seemed off somehow. Strained. Does your wife even know that we talk?

I felt guilty.

Is our friendship supposed to be a secret?

At the restaurant, your two boys were coloring and you and your wife were talking. Your wife is so pretty, and your boys are adorable. I have a son. He lives with his father in Dallas. I didn't fight for custody when we divorced. I know a mother is supposed to love her children unconditionally, but I couldn't see myself as a single parent doing any good. I stayed home with him when he was a baby and I was drowning. My whole life leaked out and "mother" filled me up. I wasn't Joan, or college graduate, not even a person anymore. Just mother. It was a sacrifice I couldn't make, but one my husband, my son, his parents, even my parents, expected me to make.

I love my son, but I never wanted children. I knew if I stayed with him, I would stop loving him and I was afraid I would hate him, or resent him, and I couldn't do that to him. Or me.

After I saw her at the restaurant, I couldn't figure out why we were talking so much. You never talk about your life at home? Why? I can't imagine how I can give you anything Suzie can't.

I miss certain things and I don't know how to get them back. I can still remember putting my hand on your shoulder while I adjusted my shoe at the gallery. I hadn't felt that safe in a long time.
Joan

From: Charles Williams <charles.williams@yahoo.com>
To: Joan Simmons <joan.simmons124@hotmail.com>
Sent: Friday, May 17, 2004 4:50 PM
Subject: Re: In sanity or out of it

Joan,

I don't talk about my home life because you offer me a break. My wife is a kind, caring woman who loves her children to distraction, but I guess I've adopted an air of weary resignation when I get home.

I'm sorry to hear about your messy divorce, but I understand. I don't think people are under any obligation to love anyone. No one thinks fathers are bad people if they don't fight for custody, and for what it's worth, I don't think you're a bad person for not fighting to keep him.

My wife doesn't know we talk. If I told her about you, it would cause trouble. Why rock the boat? You're in one scene and she's in another.

Talking to you helps me stay in sanity not out of it.
Charles

From: Joan Simmons <joan.simmons124@hotmail.com>
To: Charles Williams <charles.williams@yahoo.com>
Sent: Thursday, May 23, 2004 7:32 AM

Subject: A Health Level of Sanity

Charles,

I've come to work early every day this week meaning to e-mail back. I couldn't decide if I wanted a secret friend or not but I understand that I would upset your wife.

Not all worlds need to collide, right?

Having a husband who travels, staying home with the children—she must worry a lot. You should talk to her more often. She might enjoy hearing about crappy bands in Norman, Oklahoma who forget the words to "Freebird" (that story still cracks me up when I think about it). Stoicism is so 19th century.

Don't take my advice, though. Look what happened to my marriage.

I'm sorry for being so bitchy last Friday. I have no right to force myself into your family life. I left my husband because I needed to find myself. For the first time in my life, I think I have.

I'm glad we're friends. There's certainly no one like that in my office. Just yesterday...

* * *

Their e-mails resumed, but it was a friendship redefined by new emotions, and they were hesitant at first. They still flirted and joked, but their conversations also became more serious. Joan was frustrated by her status as "office trophy." Charles tried to comfort her and compliment her intelligence. She thanked him for treating her like a person, not a "nice rack and a heart-shaped ass like they do at work," and her emails took on a comfortable familiarity. Charles was, he noticed, a vital part of her day, and he found himself talking about dreams he used to have, places he wanted to move, and problems at home: things he used to tell Suzie back when they had time, and she seemed more sympathetic to his needs.

They e-mailed through the summer, and Charles became more and more dependent on his conversations with her. In early July, he asked Joan for her phone number and called her one Saturday from a hotel in

Amarillo, something he started doing every time he went out of town on business.

Halle Berry hadn't arrived naked at the doorstep, but Joan Simmons lingered off the porch.

* * *

It had been almost a year since they met at the museum, and Joan invited him to lunch. "Nothing celebratory, just a chance to put a face with the e-mails and phone calls," she wrote.

They decided to meet "some place where the office and our families won't collide. The last thing I want to do," she wrote, "is run through a gauntlet of clients before seeing you and eating lunch."

Strangely enough, Joan noted, they would both be in Lubbock next weekend on business.

"Suzie won't appreciate it if we car pool or share a hotel room," Charles wrote back, "but she won't care if we eat dinner together. Plus," he joked, "we'll keep it our little secret."

He got to the restaurant early, picking a table in the far back corner. When he saw her come through the door, his heart fluttered. She was dressed fashionably casual and other men watched her as she walked past their tables.

He felt the heat from her breath as he pulled her close in an embrace. The quick kiss before they sat down seemed so natural.

"It's nice to finally see you," she said, "you look like I remember."

"You got your hair cut. It looks great. You look great," he said as he reached up to touch the back of her hair, remembering that same feeling in his hands from the museum a year ago.

There was no awkwardness, and they slipped into conversation as if they were typing or talking on the phone. They lingered after the waitress removed the dishes. He ordered coffee, dragging out the moment, wondering if he was willing to carry this meeting to its logical, and perhaps inevitable, conclusion. They were on their second cup of coffee, and Charles could tell the waitress was growing impatient with them.

"Charles," Joan hesitated. "I think about you all the time. I like seeing you, hearing your voice." She wiped the table with her napkin. "We should do this more often. We could see a movie, go have some drinks at this little bar I know. My firm has offices in some of the same places you travel, and I told them last week I would be willing to work regionally. We could coordinate our schedules, meet on the road, stay in the same hotels." She paused and looked at him. "The last year, talking to you, hearing your voice... I don't want that to stop, but I want to see you. Feel your touch. I think I love you Charles, and I want us to spend our real lives together." His eyes were on the table cloth when she finished speaking.

When he looked up, Joan was smiling and she touched his hand. The restaurant was quiet, and Charles realized how few people were left in the room. The waitress stood off to the side, slyly checking her phone, probably, Charles thought, texting her boyfriend with plans for later that night. He squeezed Joan's hand and brushed her cheek with his fingers. She closed her eyes, and he realized again how perfect she seemed, but he felt something give inside. This was the sketch, frozen on the canvas of his memory, he never wanted to forget. Joan Simmons: Lubbock, TX.

Like the downtown scenes from a year ago, though, this was a moment out of context, beautiful because it was disconnected from the surrounding events.

"Everyone looks happy in their family photos," Suzie told him in the car last year. "No one takes pictures of the kids fighting on the way to the photographers. It's easy to condemn people walking past the bums in the doorways downtown, but we don't know what happened to those people that morning or the day before. We only see that snapshot in time."

Touching Joan's cheek, feeling her lips on his, would set events in motion he wasn't sure he wanted to see moving.

Charles put both hands on Joan's.

"There are times when I wonder if I'm in love with you or the idea of you. The last year has been exciting. Talking to you has been something... fresh. Suzie and I get so bogged down in the day to day there's not time anymore to dream or flirt or be free." He looked out the window. "But it's also been more than that. I love talking to you during the day, listening to your stories, and I'll admit that I've thought about us, together, without the computer. I could yell down the hall or turn over in bed to talk to you instead of staring at a screen." Charles paused and let go of her hand. "I've dreamed, more than once, about meeting you in a hotel room while I'm on the road. But then I go home and my boys hug me . . ."

Charles stared at the table as if there was an answer in the cotton threads and crumbs in front of him. Looking up took effort.

"I'm not going to let you waste your life on me, let you make a mistake you'll regret. Every time I imagine us together, I think of my boys. And my wife."

He was having a hard time looking in her eyes, knowing that there was a real danger there. For her. For him. Unsure if he could finish what he needed to say.

"I don't think I'm the answer for you. I'm afraid the happiness would fade, and I would blame you every time I missed a birthday or a little league game. God, Joan. You don't know how many times I've thought about us." Charles laughed a little. "I've dreamed about us on the beach at sunset, but then I felt guilty when I woke up. The truth is, Joan, I still love Suzie. We have a life together. It might not be perfect, but it's ours and I'm not sure I can give that up."

He looked into her eyes and knew he didn't want her to go, but her eyes sparkled with tears and her smile pierced something inside. Charles started to stand, to reach out and pull her to him, but she held her hands out in some sort of odd supplication, pushing the air down and Charles back into his seat.

"I love you, Charles." She leaned down and kissed his wet cheek, resting her hand on his shoulder. As she left, Charles noticed the waitress, standing, one hand on her phone and wiping a tear from her cheek with the other.

From: Charles Williams <charles.williams@yahoo.com>
To: Joan Simmons <joan.simmons124@hotmail.com>
Sent: September 16, 2004 7:30 AM
Subject: In or Out?

Dear Joan,

I don't want a "wife" or "the other woman." I want Joan Simmons but I can't walk away from what I've got. I meant what I said a long time ago—I admire you for knowing you can't be yourself and a mother, too. But I'm a father and a husband, and I'm not sure I can be anything else. A friend is the best I can offer.

I do need you back, though. Please write or call.

Charles

From: Mail Delivery-Subsystem
To: Charles Williams <charles.williams@yahoo.com>
Sent: September 16, 2004 7:31 AM
Subject: Returned mail: see transcript for details

The following addresses had permanent failures—
Joan Simmons <joan.simmons124@hotmail.com>

* * *

When he's on the road and spending a lonely night in some hotel after a long day, Charles still thinks about Joan, and he even googles her name once in a while. He generally gets a couple of hits that might be her—office managers at law firms in various cities—there can't be that many people named Joan Simmons out there, but he doesn't do anything. Not yet.

At home, he and his wife are still married. On Fridays they rent movies and watch the Three Stooges slap their way through another adventure. As the boys laugh, periodically trying to poke each other's eyes out, he'll pull Suzie close on the couch, put his arm around her, and feel the boy's infectious laughter. He'll watch the scene play itself out, but every once in a while, his mind will wander and he'll imagine he's at work, sitting at his desk, typing

From: Charles Williams <charles.williams@yahoo.com>
To: Joan Simmons <address unknown>
Sent: every waking moment
Subject: Hoping Our Worlds Collide Again
Dear Joan,
....

89

At the Days Inn Near Eastland

When Jill woke up with a McDonald's bag, a cake box, and an empty bottle of wine next to her, she knew something was wrong. Even more troubling were the scratchy, over-washed hotel sheets rubbing against her naked body. She hadn't slept nude since she was 12, and even then she had woken up in the middle of the night to get dressed. Lying there on this morning, Jill tried to imagine an illicit chance encounter: a bottle of wine, her naked body, and a muscle bound younger man tending to her every need, but Jill didn't feel any post-coital relaxation. Then again, she couldn't feel anything except a burning in her head, a dry mouth, and something sticky on her lips. I'm the kind of girl who likes to swallow, Jill laughed as she licked the remnants of her culinary orgy off her lips.

She slipped back into a dream about Monte Jones, her high school boyfriend. Monte had been Mr. Everything back in the day. Starting quarterback, straight-A student, and against all stereotypes, a genuinely nice guy. He was also the only real fun she had as a teen living with her Aunt, Uncle, and their five children.

When her cell phone vibrated, she opened her eyes and the world around her started spinning a half beat off from her stomach, a little like listening to Nine Inch Nails do Beethoven. As she rushed into the bathroom, Jill knew she would survive the headache, but she kind of hoped death would find her soon so her stomach would stop squirming. The phone was still making noise after rinsed her mouth.

"Hello?" Jill hated the way she sounded answering the phone. The little questioning tone at the end, unsure, a little scared. Like the next victim in a slasher movie right before she opened the cellar door, she thought. She listened, eyes closed, sitting on the edge of the bed.

"Walter. I'm okay. Stop calling. You're making my head hurt." She tossed the phone on the bed.

Jill could see her skirt and blouse strewn about the room as if cast away in some adulterous encounter. Unfortunately, Jill thought, the only thing I cheated on was my diet. She shoved the wine bottle and the cake box onto the floor and spilled back into bed, hoping Walter would give her a few minute's rest and wondering if Monte ever missed her as much as she did him.

* * *

It was supposed to be a quick trip to the store. Jill walked in at 3:47 and was in the checkout line at 4:01. Walter had called twice already, worried she would forget the organic vegetables and the red wine.

"Pesticides get in the water table and cause birth defects."

Jill mouthed the words silently as Walter spoke.

"Yes, I got the tomatoes, onion, mushrooms, and lettuce. Red leaf, organic. The wine is in the car—one of those Australian Reds and a Kendall Jackson Chardonnay of some sort, and no, they aren't the cheap stuff. Corks and everything. Look, I'm almost to the checkout line. I'll talk to you later."

As far as Jill could tell, the only difference between organic and non-organic was that one still had bugs and dirt on it. Walter's mother was convinced, though, that her sister's son was single and childless at 42 because of pesticide filled water in northern California, and Walter needed to be careful with his diet so he could keep his sperm count high. Jill didn't have the heart to tell her that Daniel was in a happy, monogamous relationship with Anthony, a History professor from UCLA. Biology, not diet, was the issue.

Her phone rang again. Some people pace when they get nervous; Walter let his fingers do the walking.

"No, I haven't forgotten the cake. I'm on my way to Halfmann's as soon as I leave the store. Have you cleaned the guest bath?" She shook her head no before Walter answered. "Okay. I'll be home in a few minutes."

Walter probably didn't remember there was a guest bath, Jill thought. She saw the woman in front of her offer a sympathetic smile—women united by incompetent husbands—there should be a union. Or a firing squad. Jill smiled back.

* * *

Jill dozed but her mind's eye was stuck at the dinner table last Christmas. She was surprised to learn, as her father-in-law carved the turkey, that she and Walter were trying to have a child, a task virtually impossible considering the tubal ligation she demanded after she miscarried a year ago. She offered to pay more for extra knots, determined never to face the possibility of childbirth again. The doctor, a middle-aged woman with long flowing hair, nodded when Jill asked her not to tell Walter.

"Of course. Men don't always understand these things," the doctor had said, but she looked at Jill as if she meant "Thank you for removing your husband from the gene pool." The look was fleeting and the doctor's face became impassive again, but Jill knew what she had seen.

After Walter's announcement, Jill struggled with her conscience. Walter looked at her like her little cousins used to when they wanted her to lie for them. In the end, she decided Christmas supper wasn't the time to tell Walter's parents that they weren't ever going to have grandchildren, that Walter repulsed her, and that they hadn't had sex in a while, something Jill didn't plan on changing anytime soon. Some nights she felt like Penelope weaving and unweaving the giant rug, but even Walter wouldn't believe she had a headache or a stomachache every night. She might be the only wife in history who encouraged her husband to look at pornography and fantasize about other women. When those options failed, she wasn't above getting Walter drunk and helping him pass out on the couch.

They had fought later that night when Walter rolled over and tried to make his earlier claim come true.

"Not tonight Walter." She pushed him away. "How could you tell your mother we're trying to have children? I told you I'm not ready after ...what happened." Jill occasionally played the trauma card. It was cruel and Jill felt vaguely dirty afterward, but, then again, it beat sex with

93

Walter.

"Jill. It's been months. I don't want to sound insensitive, but honey, I've got needs." Walter scooted his hand up and down Jill's side like he was petting a dog. He reached around, grabbed her breast and squeezed. She felt like saying "honk, honk." Very sexy, thought Jill. It's like he's checking a piece of fruit.

"My mom says a healthy sex life is important to a couple's well being. Come on. Being back home makes me feel sexy. Let me drive my train into your tunnel, baby." Walter always used this deep, throaty voice that was supposed to be cute, and according to him sexy, but it always made Jill think of trying to feed a small child who didn't want to eat her vegetables.

"It's too soon, Walter. Stop it." Jill gritted her teeth so she could shout in a whisper only Walter could hear. She slapped at his hand. "First of all it's gross having sex with your parents across the hall." She turned her face toward his. "And second of all,... Oh, forget it." She finished as her voice returned to a normal whisper and rolled over.

"What did I do wrong, Jill? Come on." He spooned himself close and started rubbing her thigh, making little thrusting motions with his pelvis, whispering "choo, choo" in her ear. "You'll feel better after we're finished. Maybe you can make a baby like mom."

Jill slapped his hand away again. "Walter," she said in a voice that didn't care who might hear, "I'm not your mother. And my tunnel is closed for repairs. Put your train back in your pants and leave me alone." She didn't tell him about her tubes. Walter was on a need to know basis.

* * *

Jill woke up when the phone vibrated again. When she sat up, her stomach followed a split second later. Jill lay back hoping to calm the furry beast threatening to explode.

"Hello? Walter, I'm okay. I'm at," she picked the pen up off the nightstand, but her head hurt too bad to read the small print, "a motel someplace east of town." Jill held the phone away from her ear. "Jesus, Walter. Don't shout. I'm sure your parents are fine without me." Jill could see Walter's father sitting in the lounge chair reading the newspaper. His mother would be standing behind him, hand on his shoulder, massaging

94

his neck. "I just needed a break. I'll call you later."

Walter wouldn't call back for a while and his mother would find a way to calm him down. The bile rose in her throat as she rolled on her side and closed her eyes.

* * *

When they first started dating in college, Jill felt lucky to find Walter. Her own parents had died when she was fourteen, and Jill had lived with an aunt and uncle. An only child at the time, Jill was unprepared to be the oldest "sister" in a house with five other siblings. At first it wasn't so bad, but Jill soon learned that a favorite aunt didn't translate into a great mother. Her uncle was a nice man, but he told her more than once that he was learning "how to parent along the way. I hope I've learned something by the time number five, uh, six is your age."

Jill knew that having a teenager was bad enough; having one thrust upon you opened up true horrors.

They did their best to treat Jill like one of their own, but she knew that the little things they couldn't afford were because of her. Shoes worn too long, clothes handed down, shorter vacations—Jill could see the relief when she left for Sam Houston State University with scholarships and a willingness to pay her own bills. Her aunt sent notes and pictures, the occasional box of cookies, but after a year or so Jill realized she was on her own. She spent the holidays and spring break in Huntsville working.

Walter's parents, on the other hand, doted on him. His apartment was filled with photographs of him with his parents or of his parents in faraway places. Most of the pictures showed both his parents, but in his guest room, Walter had various pictures of his mother posing in her swimsuit, and in a few she was clearly sunbathing topless, the camera just missing what Walter called "the naughty parts."

The first time she saw the photos, Jill asked if that was really his mother, and she could see him blush ever so slightly.

"She could have been a model for *Sports Illustrated*. Or *Playboy*," Walter added. "You have hair like hers," he said as he pulled her close, "among other things." He slid his hands down her back and traced the curve of her ass as he kissed her neck.

Jill had to admit that his mother was a beautiful woman, with a thin, youthful figure that seemed to defy gravity.

"She's had work here, here, and here," Walter said as he touched one photo with his finger. He drew a tender little circle around various parts of his mother's body. As they lay on the bed and he unbuttoned her blouse, he told her this was the room his mother stayed in when she visited.

Walter's parents still sent him care packages and spending money, even though he was a senior in college. His mother visited him regularly. A senior executive for Brown and Root since the 1960s, Walter's father had retired early, paid for his son's education, and took his wife on the occasional cruise. He had also taken up golf and various other hobbies that kept him too busy to visit, Walter told her. They had a condo in Florida back when such things seemed straight out of lifestyles of the rich and famous, and at first anyway, Jill could picture his parents holding hands, walking on white sandy beaches in exotic locations. She couldn't remember the last time she saw her aunt and uncle hold hands and her own parents were a faded memory.

Even in college, Walter had been kind of goofy, but that had been part of his charm. Monte, her only other real experience with a boy, had been a carefree lover, willing to experiment. Sex, for him, was a game and everyone should be a winner. They once had sex six times in six different places over the course of a weekend because it was their six week anniversary. We're like the devil's own kids, he joked. He liked Jill, he told her, because she didn't want to tie him down.

"I just want to have some fun and then get the hell out of this place," he said at their senior prom.

Last she heard, he went out to Stanford and, like Jill, when he left he wasn't that interested in looking backwards.

Walter, on the other hand, needed her—at first to help pass Business Communications and later to "complete his life." Back then, his flair for the romantic was touching and exciting. He was always very careful in bed, almost like he's following directions she thought one night as he slowly caressed her stomach, but she also assumed he would eventually relax and go with the flow more often. In the beginning, Walter's compliments and gifts made him seem sweet. The longer they were married, though, he seemed maudlin, like a bad black and white movie, and his gifts—earrings, dresses, lingerie—started to feel like bribes with too many strings attached.

* * *

She and Walter had been dating about a month when his parents left for the Caribbean. He took her to their house in Humble and the first weekend, they had sex in all the bedrooms, including his parents'. At the time, she felt like such a rebel, so in love, a little kinky even. Later, after they were married, Walter insisted they live near his parents so they "could house-sit when they take off."

Even living across town and married, his mother sent him gift packages, although she started addressing them to Jill. Shortly after they had moved to Humble, Jill found a gift wrapped box sitting on the front porch with her name on it. Walter was still asleep when she opened the lid to find some ginseng tea with "drink with oysters" written in black sharpie on the packaging, a *Woman's Day* article titled "10 Sex Stealers for Women" with "Sex Drive Stealer #1: Messy Bedroom" underlined twice, and a small booklet of "Sexual Positions to Increase His Pleasure: A Guide for Newlyweds." At the bottom of the box was a note from Walter's mother that said "Welcome to the neighborhood!!!! Enjoyed our stay last weekend. Let me know if you want the name of our housekeeper." Jill flipped through the booklet and noticed some of the positions were circled. Walter's mother had written things like "looks interesting" or "Walter might like this one." Jill threw everything away before Walter got up. She struggled with a thank you card.

These "little gifts" showed up periodically. Occasionally, they included homemade applesauce or fig preserves, but more often than not the gifts were more disturbing to Jill—a porn video ("to help set the mood"), lingerie ("to keep things exciting"), and once, a tube of KY Jelly ("so you don't get too sore"). Five months after they moved to Humble, Jill lobbied her company for a transfer to Abilene, hoping they would get away from her in-laws and their gift boxes.

* * *

Jill stumbled into the shower and watched the icing melt and run down her arm. Sure would be nice, Jill said to herself as she watched the water run, if the rest of her life cleaned up so easily, but she knew there wasn't enough soap in the world to wash away everything she wanted to forget. She leaned against the shower wall, feeling the sting of the water punish her for wasting Mrs. Halfmann's delicious icing, wondering if she should lie down in the tub or actually find a washcloth and clean up.

"Big party tonight, Mrs. Childress?"

"Just my in-laws, Mrs. Halfmann." Jill looked up from her checkbook. "Sometimes it hardly seems worth the effort, don't you think?"

"Especially when it's the in-laws." Mrs. Halfmann looked toward the back. "Mr. Halfmann's mother was a trial, god rest her soul." She made the sign of the cross and kissed her thumb. "Some days, it was all I could do to be civil to that woman." She leaned across the counter and whispered. "I can't tell you how many times I went to the grocers and almost didn't come back. If not for the kids... ." Mrs. Halfmann gave a little wave. "Water under the bridge, right? Have a nice time, dear. I'll pray it's a short visit."

Jill sat in the car. The cake smelled delicious, and she had skipped lunch so she could run errands. As she put the car into reverse, she could see Mr. Halfmann come out of the back room and move right behind Mrs. Halfmann, putting his hands on her hips. She slapped at his hands, a pained smile on her lips as he leaned forward and whispered something in her ear. Jill saw Mrs. Halfmann shaking her head but being led to the backroom.

Turning onto the freeway instead of heading straight home wasn't as difficult as she thought it might be. Traffic was light and whatever moral dilemma she anticipated went away when she rolled down the windows and turned the radio up. She sang, ignoring the ringing cell phone.

Jill had turned onto the highway at 5:07 singing with John Mellencamp. She and Monte used to pretend they were Jack and Diane, slipping off her Bobby Brooks so he could do what he pleased. "You know, I'm really into you," he would tell her every once in a while right before they had sex, "especially now" he would add as he slid in.

Jill told herself she was going to drive around and clear her head before heading home when Simon & Garfunkel's "Mrs. Robinson" came on the radio. The station was ten minutes into their "5 O'Clock Fast Lane: 30

Minutes of Classic Rock to Get You Home," and Jill decided Walter could live without her for a little while longer. Her phone was ringing on a pretty regular basis now, and she smiled while she was singing "Koo-Koo-Ka-Choo," thinking about the slow panic creeping into Walter's face. He was always trying to impress his parents and please his mother, a woman, Jill doubted, Jesus would love more than she could know. If at all.

She pulled over on the shoulder. The ringing was distracting her from the music, and Jill hated to drive while she talked.

"Walter you don't have to keep calling and asking when I'll be home. I've got the cake..." She lifted the pink lid on the box. "It looks delicious." She swiped her finger across the icing. "Tastes good too. I'll hurry. Should be home soon." She put the phone down, opened the glove box and found a little plastic spoon. "Take that Martha Stewart," she said as she took a bite of the cake. She looked at the bottle of wine and wondered if carrot cake went better with red or white wine. A semi drove by, rattling the car as she took another bite. She got back on the highway, fully intending to turn around and go home.

* * *

The cold water woke her up. Jill was curled up at the back of the tub, chilled to the bone and shaking as she reached forward to turn the water off. She had forgotten to shampoo her hair, and she could see the water dripping off the ends as she dried off, but she didn't think she had the energy to turn the water back on even if there was hot water.

She and Walter had been dating a short time when he took her home to meet his parents for the first time. There was a note on the table telling them that his father was out playing golf. They assumed his mother was at the store or out running other errands. Walter smiled at her, leading her upstairs, telling her they had time for a "quickie" before anyone got home. Halfway up they heard the shower, and Walter looked back and shrugged, surprised that someone was home. Jill stopped, expecting to go back downstairs and wait, but Walter kept walking. "Come on," he whispered. "We have time before she finishes." Jill was having none of it. First impressions mattered to her, and she headed back down.

"I'll tell her we are here, okay." Jill wandered around downstairs. When Walter came down, Jill tried not to notice that the ends of his hair were wet.

* * *

At about 5:30, Jill turned her ringer off and put the phone on vibrate. Walter had called again, wondering when Jill "thought she might show up."

"Soon, Walter." Jill noticed the sign for I-20 East and changed lanes.

"That's what you said 20 minutes ago." Walter shouted and for a fleeting moment, Jill felt a little sorry for him. He never hit her, rarely yelled, and didn't call her stupid names like honey or dear when he was upset. One time he did call her "mommy" when she was pregnant and he was rubbing her neck, letting his hands slide down her arms so his fingers "accidentally" brushed against her breasts. It was about as smooth as Walter could be and when they first started dating, she found that kind of clumsiness endearing. That morning she threw up and told him not to call her that ever again.

"Walter, I was visiting with Mrs. Halfmann..."

Walter interrupted her. "Jill, I don't care. My mother will be here in a few minutes, and the bathroom isn't clean. The food's in your car. And you aren't here."

Jill saw a Pinkie's Liquor store just beyond the next exit.

"I just remembered that our corkscrew doesn't work very well." Jill slowed down to exit. "I'm pulling into a liquor store to get a new one. I'll be home when I get there, Walter. You know," Jill added as she turned the car off, "you could have cleaned the bathroom yourself."

Corkscrew in hand, Jill sat in her car. Her phone vibrated against the cake box, and she dropped it in her purse as she grabbed the spoon to take another bite, wishing she had some milk. Her eyes rested on the wine bottles. The sign by the door warned her that consuming alcoholic beverages right here was illegal, but Jill had a vague memory of her father coming out of a store with two cups of ice and a bottle of whiskey. It was odd considering she had so few memories of her parents. In her vision of him, he was happy and he gave Jill a piece of ice before he opened the bottle and poured whiskey into the cups. She heard her mother laugh and saw her parents toast each other but that was where the memory ended. Jill found an old Whataburger cup, opened the Chardonnay, and poured herself a drink, offering a silent toast to the parents she wished she could remember. As she drank, the clerk looked at her and smiled, raising his hand in what Jill wanted to believe was a blessing for her choice. She backed out and merged onto the interstate, the sun in her rearview mirror.

* * *

Jill shivered as she walked across the hotel room to her clothes, wishing she could simply choose what to remember and what to forget. The second bottle of wine was in the trash with her pantyhose thrown carelessly on top of it. At least the maid will have something to talk about, she thought. She picked up her cell phone and dialed the home number

"Hello?"

"Mr. Childress. Is Walter there?"

"Jill? Boy am I glad you called. Walter has been worried sick." There was a pause. "Um. Listen Jill, Walter is upstairs right now. I think Martha went up to help calm him down. Should I have him call you back?"

Jill sat there looking at the curtains.

"Jill? Jill, are you there?"

"I'm still here, Mr. Childress. Would you please tell Walter," she picked her keys up off the bed and started walking toward the door, "he can come get the organic vegetables at the Days Inn near Eastland if he still wants them."

Without waiting for an answer, Jill dropped her phone on top of the pantyhose as she walked out the door.

Coitus Interruptus

The day Bill Wheatley got a letter from Kim Novak, a woman he'd dated over a year ago, he had no idea what to expect. The breakup had been messy, and, admittedly, a little disturbing. "The sex was great, but she wanted a little more commitment than I was willing to offer. Plus," he told a friend from work, "why buy the cow, when you can get the milk for free every Friday night around town? I'm not saying the woman was crazy," he added, "but she hadn't seen normal in a few years, if you know what I mean."

The truth was that when Bill wanted sex, he went out.

"Human interaction," a professor told him in college, "is another type of transaction. You can become friends with anyone if you can convince them you're a product worth investing in. Life is all about marketing: accentuate the positive and distract from the negative."

Bill doubted the old guy was offering dating advice, but he realized early on he could apply his skills as a marketing and ad designer to the bar scene. There was always a willing partner at some local pub: she just didn't know it yet. Bill would find a booth near the wall and survey the field. Focus on the unexpected—compliment her hair, hands, shoes, earrings, ankle bracelets—anything but what all the other men were staring at that night. Always stroke the erogenous zones with words first, Bill thought.

"How are you tonight?" Bill would ask, sliding next to a likely customer. After some perfunctory small talk, Bill might tell her "I noticed your shoes as I was walking over. Are those Prada or Manolo Blahnik?

Either way, you have beautifully shaped ankles." Bill knew just enough about women's fashion to be dangerous.

He always offered a firm handshake, looked her in the eyes, avoided her chest. He'd been watching it already. The goal was to make her to feel safe and in control.

When she spoke, no matter what she said, Bill listened, letting her know he cared about her. He was a man, he wanted her to think, seeking a connection and trying to avoid the meat market bar scene, here because it was hard to "meet women in the produce section at the grocery store."

If there was a lull in the conversation, Bill would hold out his hand and touch her ear. "Those are beautiful earrings. They complement your hair perfectly." As he said it, he let his fingers linger on her ear lobe and brush against her neck. It was an attention to detail that most women wanted and many men couldn't provide. Inevitably, when Bill was ready, they went back to his apartment to "talk in private, where the music isn't so loud." He didn't spend many Friday nights alone.

But things happen we don't always expect. Kim wrote that she'd quit her job and emptied her bank account to pay for a trip to Florida. She wasn't writing to "brag about my early retirement and make you jealous, though." In a fit of panic, "a kind of mid-life crisis" she wrote, Kim reexamined her life and found it lacking. At 26, she worked a dead-end job for an insurance company underwriting policies. Everything she learned as an English major at SMU seemed irrelevant, and she spent her work day undoing four years of her very expensive college education. She wanted to wipe the slate clean. So she headed for Florida and, while sitting on the beach drinking up her savings account one Mai Tai at a time, she decided to work on a Masters Degree and Ph.D.

As part of this fresh start, she had begun an exercise program, stopped drinking ("except socially, of course"), and had a complete physical. She was writing because during the physical, the doctor asked if she was sexually active and if she had "multiple partners" within the last two years. While it was tempting to lie—"I didn't want him to think I was a slut," she joked with little ha ha's in parenthesis—she told the truth. Kim hadn't taken the HIV test yet, but her doctor suggested she get one soon. She'd been feeling pretty run down and achy lately. Based on her "personal history," the doctor was worried she was "at-risk. Of course, I could also have the flu or be suffering from too many drinks in the hot sun. Ha. Ha."

Bill wasn't that amused.

"I'm writing all my friends, not to scare them or anything," but to touch base with anyone she had "been with recently (and often wink, wink)" and to let them know "what was up."

Bill crumpled her letter and threw it across the room. He dressed and called a cab.

Bill kept replaying bits and pieces of their relationship as he got ready to go out. He had broken off with her when she grew increasingly game oriented in bed. Or, out of bed, as it were. Bill liked to add a little spice to his bedroom fare as much as the next guy: dressing in a tweed jacket while the desperate student came begging for a higher grade; pretending to be a hospital patient attended by the horny nurse; boss and secretary—fun and games where the means enhanced the end, but after a couple of months of pretty good sex, things got out of hand.

The three times Bill and Kim had unprotected sex had been spontaneous moments near the end of their relationship—in a darkened movie theater full of other people, in a public restroom at Nordstroms, and at a construction site where Kim laid on a nail that punctured her ass. When she stood up afterwards and showed him the blood, he asked why she hadn't said anything. She laughed and told him the pain made the orgasm that much more intense. He refused to kiss it and make it better, but he did suggest she get a tetanus shot.

After the nail incident, Bill insisted they restrict themselves to indoor activities. Kim seemed bored so Bill rented *Flashpoint X* one night. He'd read in *GQ* that watching porn together could spice up a couple's sex life.

"It's like *Backdraft*, except the firefighters light fires instead of just putting them out," he read on the DVD case.

She seemed skeptical at first, but after a pretty hot night in bed, she was hooked. The next few weeks, she stopped at the video store before coming to the apartment so they could watch the movie then perform the scenes. Bill was enjoying himself until the night she showed up wearing a man's suit carrying a movie called *Debbie's Boys*.

"I brought this dress for you to wear," she told him.

Bill put on the dress and watched the movie, but he drew the line when she pulled out a giant pink dildo and a tube of KY jelly. Some of his neighbors still won't talk to him after seeing him wearing panty hose, a poorly fitting bra, and throwing a red dress after Kim as she ran screaming down the hall.

Over the next few days, his voice mail filled with the oddly flattering rage of a woman scorned, but when she left a mobile made with pornographic dvds and used condoms on his apartment door handle with the words "Call me, you cunt" in red lipstick, he changed his phone number and told the doorman of his building to stop letting her in. He hadn't heard from her since.

Bill paid the cab driver and walked into the Oasis, hoping his memories of Kim would go away with a drink and the first beautiful woman he saw.

"I'll take a seven and seven," he told the bartender before turning around. He caught sight of a beautiful brunette brushing her hair off her ear. She was talking, or rather listening, to some guy pointing to the stage, but the way she stood, half turned to leave, told Bill they weren't together. She nodded once and walked toward the bar.

"That is a beautiful bracelet. Lagos or Alexis Bittar?" Bill held his hand out, resting it on the bar. "Do you mind if I look at it closer?"

The brunette smiled at him.

"It was a gift from my mother." She held out her wrist.

Bill's left hand stayed open, but he moved his right hand over toward the bracelet, touching it and moving against the top of her hand. "Is this amethyst?" He looked up at her eyes. "I'll bet that's your birthstone." As he said this, he took her hand and held it between both of his: "I'm Bill, by the way, bracelet connoisseur and jewelry admirer."

"Kelly Cattrell. Nice to meet you."

"Kelly, I just got off work and I would be honored if a beautiful woman would let me buy her a drink." He stood and signaled to the bartender.

He looked at Kelly with his eyebrows slightly arched.

"White wine," she said.

Bill found a small table toward the back corner of the bar. "Would you like to sit, talk a bit?" As he said it, he already had his right hand on her back, and he was gently applying pressure with his fingers. Three drinks later, Kelly Cattrell, Assistant Design Editor for a local non-profit magazine, and Bill were in the cab. As they rode to his apartment, he imagined her naked and crawling on top of him as he cradled her hips.

"Would you like another glass of white wine?" Bill asked as he opened the door.

"Maybe one more. But only half a glass."

Kim's letter was still crumpled on the floor near the couch. He picked up the letter and shoved it in his pocket apologizing for the mess.

"I'll get the wine."

In the kitchen, he fumbled with the cork screw and dropped a wine glass, catching it before it shattered on the floor. He could feel Kim's letter in his pocket.

When he handed Kelly her wine, her hand lingered on his, and they kissed. Bill steered them toward the bedroom. Standing behind her, he unbuttoned her dress letting his fingers rest ever so slightly on each button and brushing his lips against her neck. As he leaned against her, he felt the paper press against his thigh. His hands froze on Kelly's shoulders before he could refocus, moving closer, nuzzling her neck, reaching around to massage her breasts.

She turned to face him and as they kissed she unbuckled his belt. He felt Kim's letter slide down his leg, and his erection seemed to slide with it. Bill lay on the bed and watched as Kelly crawled toward him. She looked at him, lying there, flaccid.

"What's wrong? Do we need a little motivation?" and she took him in her mouth.

But Bill didn't see Kelly. He saw Kim.

And he saw Kim's letter.

And nothing happened.

Kelly left Bill lying on his bed, limp, pathetic, embarrassed. She called for a taxi while he lay there thinking about Kim.

Mostly he thought about the letter. HIV. AIDS. Bill got up and walked to the shower, wondering who he would write to if Kim tested positive.

"At least Kelly's safe," he told himself as the hot water washed over him.

When he was in college, Bill's sister found out she was pregnant. Afraid to tell her husband, she had Bill drive her to the clinic and pretend to be Greg. During the visit, the doctor asked if they wanted to test the baby for Down's Syndrome and other diseases. Before Rosalind could answer, the doctor asked, point blank, if she had any thoughts about aborting the baby. "If you know you're going to keep the baby, don't take the test," he said. "If the baby's abnormal, you'll have your whole life to deal with it. Why add seven extra months of mental anguish?"

Bill, thinking more about Kim now than when they dated, wasn't sure if he wanted to know the results of her test. Ignorance is bliss and he wasn't sure the truth would set him free.

He stopped going out, though, working longer hours and coming home more and more tired. Never a big tv fan, he found himself spending his evenings surfing the web at home. Initially, he spent time on medical sites researching HIV, AIDS, and other sexually transmitted diseases, but his web searches created a chain reaction. Web ads for penile enhancement, neighborhood "fuck buddies," even a few religious web sites offering to help save his soul popped up during his searches. He started receiving emails reminding him that the best way to avoid an STD was through "Safe, Virtual Sex."

"As long as your hand is clean, you'll be safe," one site advertised.

At first he ignored the spam, but the e-mails from free porn sites, "See J-Lo nude," "Visit the Isle of Lesbian Love," lingered longer and longer in his in-box, and occasionally before deleting the messages, he clicked on the link for curiosity's sake. He read once that without pornography, the internet would be an economic disaster and shrivel up. Kind of like my sex life, he thought.

After a while, Bill took a sort of professional interest in the technology of pornography. He convinced himself that any good marketer would want to know how this industry can make so much money. People complain, but this stuff was obviously working. At least, that's what Bill told himself.

Over these first couple of weeks, Bill limited himself to searching just once after work. Each evening, with some trepidation, he checked the mail box for a letter from Kim. Letting his worries slip away into the cyber void, Bill settled in to his computer chair, loosened his belt and began to surf. He avoided the hard core stuff. Women with horses, gang bangs, women whose breasts were the size of small cars—Bill could never figure out who enjoyed that stuff. Women with other women, on the other hand. Or women touching themselves. Movie stars. The internet allowed him to remove the mystery—Jennifer Anniston looked even better without clothes, even if the pictures were grainy and far away.

Some days he just looked, other days he would stroke himself without even thinking about it. The first time, he found himself running to the bathroom. He was more careful in the future: leaving the computer earlier, keeping a rag handy, moving the trash can closer. Periodically, he glanced around the room with a guilty look on his face. He felt like a kid again, staring at the bra section of the JC Penny's Catalogue while his parents were out of the house. Each day, he vowed to stop, but, inevitably, he sat at the computer after coming home.

Within a month, all pretense was gone. After work, Bill went home, found his site of the day and consummated the act. Photos can only tell part of the story, though, and he found himself wanting more action. He tried some amateur sites that showed real women doing strange things in public, horny neighbors, and lonely housewives, but he didn't want real women. A real woman had caused all this trouble in the first place. It didn't help that one of the MILFs he saw looked suspiciously like his Aunt Katie. That would sure spice up the next family reunion, Bill thought.

Late one night, almost by accident, he found Shiva Touché and her streaming videos. She was clean, evenly tanned with long blond hair, and she could dance. Tantalizingly. With great talent and flexibility, Bill noticed. No danger of HIV here. Bill downloaded the necessary drivers and, for the first time, he used his credit card and got his own password. Shiva was all his, willing to send personalized emails when she posted new videos "just for him." She became a part of his daily life and evening routine.

Until Kim's letter, Bill had managed to keep his private life and work life separate. Spellman Advertising wasn't ever going to make him rich, but the perks and salary provided what he needed for a comfortable life.

"Marketing is a good job," one of his professors told him at a graduation party, "if you can keep your zipper up at the office."

Bill steadfastly followed this advice, but he found himself less and less able to focus at work. Recently, he had landed the McMahon Dry Cleaning Campaign, but his creative juices had dried up faster than his sex life.

Sitting at his desk one morning, the McMahon Dry Cleaner folder on his desk, Bill stared at the computer thinking of Shiva. He told himself he would take a quick peak to get the creative juices flowing. Since his door was already shut, Bill simply turned the lock, or thought he turned the lock, and sat back down. Leaving his pants buttoned and his shirt tucked in, Bill called up Shiva's web page and saw her smiling, running her fingers through her hair, and he pictured the perfect commercial.

Shiva could walk in the store, empty handed. Her hair would flow back in the breeze and her body would be silhouetted under the dress. She was no frumpy housewife frazzled by the daily grind. The clerk would ask if he could help her and Shiva, in a sultry voice dripping with unrealized sexual desire, would say "I need my dress cleaned. Can you do it while I wait?" As she spoke, she would be unbuttoning her yellow summer dress and as the "t" in "wait" faded, her dress would slip to the floor. His hand slid into his lap as he watched Shiva on the computer screen and imagined her walking around the counter and into his arms.

He never head the door open.

Caught in *flagrante delicto* with a streaming video of Shiva Touché crawling toward him, right shoulder forward, lips opened ever so slightly, licking her red, lush lips—Bill thought he was surprisingly calm when the custodian screamed. By the time Mr. Spellman rushed in to his office, Bill had put everything away, so to speak, but Mrs. M. Perez painted a pretty clear picture of what she had seen.

Bill wanted to look ashamed while his boss talked, but what could he say: I was practicing safe sex? Brainstorming ideas? Doing market research? It beats stealing pens? He could claim Mrs. Perez was exaggerating and hadn't seen anything, but he had too much pride for that.

"Because the nature of the case is a first for the company, we've decided to review your employee folder, check company liability issues, and make a decision tomorrow. For today, I think it best that you go on home, but leave your current project out on your desk," Spellman coughed into his hand, embarrassed. "Leave your password, also. The technician will check your work log." Spellman closed his eyes, and Bill almost felt sorry for him. "Anyway, I'd like you to come in tomorrow morning at 9:30 so we can meet again. Do you have any questions?"

"No sir. I would just like to say I'm sorry for what happened." How does one apologize for whacking off at the office, Bill wondered? He needed Dear Abby on this one. Or maybe Dr. Ruth.

The conversation the next day with Spellman was short. Because his record was clean, and "if you can assure me this will never happen again," Spellman would give Bill another chance. Bill quickly assured Mr. Spellman of his new found cyber celibacy and went to his office. He didn't make much progress on the McMahon Dry Cleaning ad, but he also managed to avoid any more embarrassing moments at work. Mrs. M. Perez refused to enter his office and she insisted he empty his own trash, but that was a small price to pay, he thought.

When the letter from Kim arrived, Bill didn't find a note detailing his imminent death, but a bookmark with a biblical passage and a long letter from his newly "saved" ex-girlfriend in Florida. She told Bill that as she left the HIV test, she had a vision and in that vision God spoke to her, telling her she was truly blessed and that her body was cleansed of its sins. When her test came back negative, she knew her revelation had been true. As a tribute to the "glorious King of Kings," Kim said she was dedicating her life to spreading the word of God to all her friends. At the end of the letter, she passed on her blessings and urged him to drop on his knees and pray for forgiveness. Never particularly religious, Bill did offer a silent thank you to Jesus. HIV free. He had nothing to worry about. Time to shut the computer down and find a real, live woman, Bill thought.

Filled with a sense of renewal, he walked past the computer chair with only a momentary glance. He dressed with care and took a cab to his favorite pub. After a light sandwich, a few drinks and a survey of the terrain, Bill felt confident, like his old self, but the women all had flaws. Kelly Cattrell stood across the room. "No wonder I couldn't get it up. Look at that nose," Bill thought. "And that woman with her—what's up with her hair."

Where were the smooth, silky women who used to come here, Bill wondered as he went home disappointed and alone. Walking in the apartment, he saw his computer. He thought of Shiva, but he went to bed instead, thinking that night was a temporary setback.

"I'll get back on that horse tomorrow," he told himself. I just hope I find a woman who doesn't look like a horse, he thought as he crawled under the covers.

The earlier high from Kim's letter was gone. He spent a sleepless night wondering if Shiva missed him as much as he missed her. To avoid temptation, Bill started going to various bars directly after work each day, but each time he came home alone, earlier and earlier each night. Breaking up was hard to do, but Bill kept telling himself all he needed was the warm touch of a woman's body to pull him out of his funk.

Without Shiva to get him through the nights, though, Bill lost his focus. Two weeks after Kim's letter, he found himself lonely and tired staring at his computer at work. He had a note from Shiva in his inbox wondering if he was experiencing any technical difficulties and reminding him he was paid through the end of the month. She had "uploaded a bonus video just for him," but he needed to act fast. "This one's so hot it's burning up the web," Shiva wrote.

He sat at his desk and tried to focus on the McMahon ad campaign. Earlier in the week, Bill had pitched the basic design for his commercial to Spellman. It was a much cleaner version—he kept the voice but lost the nudity—than the one Mrs. M. Perez had interrupted. Spellman had offered a few suggestions and given him the go ahead to sketch out the video shoot, create a list of actors, and budget the cost.

Bill knew he needed an actress who was tall with distinctive features that would stand out in a shadow shot. Shiva Touché would be perfect, Bill thought as he sketched her in. Before he realized it, Bill had storyboards for his commercial, including his role as the helpful clerk who shows Shiva how her dress will be cleaned. It was, he told himself, inspired stuff.

As he leaned back in his chair, he wondered how tall Shiva was and if she was available for commercials. After all, she was a professional actress. Of sorts. Spellman didn't need to know what kind of actress. A quick look at the web site for professional research purposes seemed appropriate. Better close the door, though, just in case anyone wanders by, Bill told himself. We can't afford any more mistakes, he muttered toward the computer as he walked to the door. He turned the lock, silently cursed Mrs. M. Perez, and slid his extra chair up under the door knob, welcoming Shiva back into his life. But only on a professional basis, he told himself as he sat down and slid his hand into his lap.

Dear Search Committee

It should have been an easy letter to write. Nathan Dumbrowski had been teaching for about 10 years, and he was a leader in his department and a confidante of various administrators.

Dear Search Committee:
I write with great interest in your recently advertised Head, Department of English position, fully recognizing that my interest in your job will probably exceed your interest in me. My years of experience teaching and my record of working with colleagues to improve programs and recruit and retain students should qualify me for such a position, but I suspect my reward is in heaven instead of a bigger office with a larger paycheck and less work. But, what the hell, right? It's Friday afternoon, and I can either grade functionally illiterate essays written by students perpetually on probation, surf the internet for free porn, or apply to be a Department Head.

Nathan considered his opening gambit. He also decided surfing the web for porn sounded like a good idea.
Nathan wasn't necessarily unhappy in his job. Tenured and recently divorced, he had a unique combination of job security and personal freedom that most people would envy. Even so, he increasingly had thoughts, some romantic and some pornographic, about various students and one night after drinking too many White Russians, a colleague in his department. Talking to her in the hall the next day, he wondered about his sanity. And his eyesight.

In my ten years of teaching at the university level, I have taught two freshman composition courses each semester, throwing my energies into explaining thesis sentences and paragraph structure to over 1000 first year students, reading 5000 essays that equal, roughly, 150,000 pages and utilize around 10 million words—words often strung together with a narrative complexity that rivals the most difficult passages in James Joyce's *Finnegan's Wake*. Solving that complexity is the mission I embark on each semester. Our goal, quite frankly, is to touch our students' lives...

"And sometimes their bodies," Nathan whispered. He needed to get ready for class, and the letter wasn't going that well.

"Honesty isn't always the best policy," he told his composition students the first day of class each semester. "Tell your girlfriend you love romantic comedies, let your roommate think he's smarter than you, and give your parents hope you might someday graduate."

Nathan would pause to allow a slight chuckle from the good students before turning serious.

"But let's remember, as Marcus Aurelius tells us, to 'Live a good life. If there are gods and they are just, then they will not care how devout you have been, but will welcome you based on the virtues you have lived by.'"

Nathan would look around the room.

"Our goal in this world is to live what Aurelius would call a 'noble life that will live on in the memories of our loved ones.' Your writing can be a record of that life, the articulation of your ideas. At the risk of sounding melodramatic, what we write is a reflection of who we are and who we might become. We develop that sense of self if we are willing to be ruthless, brutal, and honest when we look in the mirror each morning and when we read the words we put on the page."

Nathan delivered the opening speech, moving around the room, hoping to inspire his students to see writing as something more than using commas correctly.

"But," he told a colleague, "half my students think Marcus Aurelius is a running back for the Green Bay Packers, and the other half are pretty sure I gave them permission to lie to their girlfriends."

Nathan was convinced, after reading ten million words, many of them definitely not (or defiantly not as his spell-check averse students might write) a reflection of anything but late night typing binges, that there were fewer and fewer students who cared about learning.

"They keep telling us we need to create life-long learners," he said last summer after a professional development seminar. "I'd settle for 50-minute learners. It's like talking to a room of potted plants. They're all looking for quick and easy, and we're peddling long and complicated."

Late last semester, he was in the office Sunday evening when he had a knock on the door.

"Professor Dumbrowski?"

He looked up from his most recent stack of papers. Erica Jenkins was a student in his second semester freshman class, and she was that rare writer who could construct grammatically clean sentences that made absolutely no sense. She was also fond of short skirts and tank tops with spaghetti straps, he noted early in the semester.

"Erica." Nathan looked up. "What are you doing roaming the halls of academe on a Sunday evening?"

"I was in the computer lab upstairs working on our next essay." Erica looked up and down the hallway. "Grading papers?"

"Yes." Nathan wasn't in the visiting mood. He had thirteen essays left, and he shifted his eyes to the stack and then back at Erica, hoping she might get the hint.

"I've learned *so* much in your class." Erica stood with her hands on the door frame. She was backlit by the hall light, her right knee bent as she leaned forward ever so slightly. Coquettishly, he thought.

"But I'm *really* not doing well." She hesitated, pulling her hands off the door frame. "It's like I can't figure out what you want from us."

Nathan noticed the strap from her purse pulling her shirt tightly across her chest. Her eyes glowed.

"I was wondering, if you aren't too busy, if you could maybe help me with my paper?" She gave him a coy smile. "I would be *so* grateful if you could. God, I would do just about *anything* for a good grade in this class."

Nathan noticed the way her hip curved out toward the door, the flush of her cheeks.

"Come on in," Nathan said. "And shut the door so we don't get interrupted."

Touching lives indeed.

Education experts tell us that our students are changing, and we must engage them with technology and help them become active learners. Many of our students, they say, see education as a task to complete before they enter the "real" world. Administrators and faculty members, too often, overreact to such pronouncements. Universities create Faculty Development Centers and hold workshops, training sessions, and Lunch and Learns that focus on pedagogy, methodology, and a bunch of other "ologies" no one heard of ten years ago and not many people understand today. The Department Head must be ready and willing to step in and remind faculty that the single most important teaching tool we can bring to the classroom is passion—for our subject, our scholarship, and, most importantly, for our good looking students.

Nathan stared at his shadowed image on the computer screen, fingers resting on the keyboard, curious, in many ways, what he might type next.

Before his divorce, Nathan's passion for teaching and scholarship was, he admitted, stellar. He enjoyed watching students come alive in his classes, and he worked late hours reading and helping students. They were, he told his wife, charges entrusted to him by parents and society. When he wasn't helping students, he was engaged in his own scholarship: nothing flashy and no major publications but good, workmanlike production that earned him a decent reputation, raises, and admiration from colleagues, administrators, and faculty. When he talked to students about the life of the mind, Nathan imagined himself as a modern day Socrates, a kind of public intellectual, helping to shape the future one student at a time.

Nathan had vowed when he was an undergraduate to avoid the pitfalls of middle-class America, rejecting the simplistic blue collar politics of his parents while embracing complexity and contextuality. Reading Flaubert's *Madame Bovary* and Cormac McCarthy's *Blood Meridian* as a sophomore had a strange, transformative effect on his life, causing him to look back on his tawdry upbringing, seeing his parents as backward hicks. Ignorant. Uneducated. He wanted to offer his students the same type of insight and opportunities.

Going to graduate school had been an easy decision for him but one that made no sense to his parents. The truth was they thought college itself was a waste of time.

"Bill Cases' boy went. Took some classes, smoked some dope, and he ended up right back at the plant. There ain't nothing a college education can do for you that working with your hands won't do. Waste of time and money. I can get you on right after graduation," his father told him when he was a senior in high school, "but we're not throwing money away so you can go off and forget where you come from."

"I try to forget a little more each day, you old bastard," Nathan thought, sitting in front of his computer.

Between financial aid and working, Nathan managed to struggle along, poor but doing well. He came home during the holidays the first three years, mostly so he could see his friends, but he hadn't seen his parents since his senior year of college when his dad called Bill Clinton a pussy-whipped faggot.

"He was probably a English major," he sneered and Nathan's mother laughed.

Nathan finished eating and went up to his room to pack. Posters, a few ribbons, and the odd memento from trips that usually ended about like supper that night: Nathan looked around the room surrounded by a childhood he couldn't un-remember. When he left later that night, he packed light, hoping whatever he left would stay where it belonged.

They did call when he graduated with his undergraduate degree. He had mailed them a graduation announcement, putting it in the mail the Monday after he walked the stage.

"We got that letter about graduation. I worked a double this weekend so we wouldn't have made it anyway."

He could picture his parents sitting at the kitchen table, a couple of glasses near their elbows, whiskey bottle off to the side.

"I can still get you that job," his dad said, "but I need to know if you're willing to start at the bottom."

He could hear his dad take a drink.

"Sometimes you college boys think you're too good for hard work."

When he told his dad he was planning on going to graduate school, there was a long pause. "He says he's goin' to graduate school." His dad had the phone held away from his mouth, but Nathan still couldn't hear his mother's response.

"Hell and goddamn, boy. You already got the B.S. You know what M.S. and PhD mean, right?"

Nathan could picture his dad's lip curling. His mother was smiling and, probably, taking a long drink.

"An M.S. is more shit and a PhD just means you can pile it higher and deeper."

There wasn't anything for Nathan to say, but he could hear his dad laughing to himself.

"Well, that job won't be waitin' for you. No sir. I can't hold it that long. Let us know when you get tired of living in that Ivory Tower and wanna get a real job."

Nathan started to speak but his dad told him to keep in touch, and he heard the ice cubes rattle in the glass as the line went dead. They hadn't spoken since.

"Thomas Wolfe said you can't go home again," he told his wife right before they got married, "and I, for one, am grateful. I decided a long time ago that I wasn't going to trip on what's behind me."

So far, he had managed to do so. He was, at the relatively young age of 42, a tenured, full Professor. Of course, that and $3.50 will get you a cup of coffee these days, Nathan said when he got his letter from the university president, but small consolations are better than none at all he used to tell himself. He also knew that he had made a difference in the lives of his students. Nathan received Christmas cards and, on occasion, phone calls and emails updating him on their successes. These were important, intangible rewards that helped keep him working late.

Before his wife left, he was nominated for a major teaching award. He didn't win, but, he told her, it was an honor to have a chance. He wasn't sure she believed him, and he wasn't sure he believed himself.

"I can't do any more than I'm already doing," he told her in a rare moment of self pity. "If that isn't enough, then..." He waved his hand and moved on.

The job of a Department Head is not radically different from that of a faculty member. Much like faculty, the Head must manage and facilitate understanding among a variety of constituents while remembering the larger goals of the classroom, the department, and the university. In the classroom, each student has his or her own interests and desires. Good teachers help students connect the course content with short and long term goals. Likewise, faculty have disparate research agendas and teaching styles. The Head must, like a good teacher, find a way to bring those various interests and abilities together. He sees himself as a leader, a man Fred Exley writes in his brilliant fictional memoir *A Fan's Notes*, who "comes to imagine that his female trusts spend half their nocturnal hours masturbating to his summarily called-up and glamorized image."

Probably not the best quote about teaching, Nathan thought. In fact, Exley's not the guy to quote about much of anything unless it's a suicide letter. Professional or otherwise. Nathan leaned back in his chair.

When his wife told him she was leaving, Nathan wasn't surprised. Standing near the car trunk full of boxes and clothes, she complained that she always felt like there was a second Nathan lurking under the surface, hidden by the extra hours at work.

"You're here, but you've never fully committed." She put her last suitcase in the trunk. "Even worse, Nathan. You come home, eat, have a drink, and read or grade. You don't seem to want kids anymore, you abandoned your parents, and we don't even have very many friends. It's pretty obvious you don't want me." She looked up over his shoulder. "You've always worked hard, but there's something different. You used to enjoy it, but now..." She shrugged her shoulders and started getting in the car. "There are these firewalls, and it's like, I don't know, like you've spent your whole life proving you aren't your parents." She was sitting looking up at him. Nathan had his hand on the top of the door. "Well. You've done it, but there's more to life than proving you aren't someone else. At some point, you have to let go of who you aren't and actually be someone." She pulled the door closed and backed down the driveway.

Nathan went in the house, made a drink, and stood by the front window fairly certain she wouldn't like the real him either.

119

They had met in graduate school. Nathan was about halfway through chapter three of his dissertation when his computer screen at work turned blue. The student worker at the IT Help Desk told him he had the "blue screen of death," and he must have heard the growing panic in Nathan's voice. "We'll get someone over right away," he added quickly.

Nicole was there within 15 minutes, and Nathan breathed a sigh of relief when he saw his chapter appear on the screen. He asked her out that day, and they were married a year later in front of a Justice of the Peace. A few friends from school attended as witnesses but that was about it. Her parents had died two years before in a car accident, and neither Nathan nor Nicole had particularly deep ties to anyone in their extended families. They both graduated in May. He got the tenure track job, and she started working as an IT Specialist on campus, rising to Chief Security Officer before she left for a better position when they divorced.

As he stood by the window, Nathan could track the collapse of their marriage relatively easily. When they were first married, they spent their vacations and weekends traveling and taking up various hobbies. Their photo albums were filled with sky diving, snorkeling, biking trips in foreign countries, and even a hunting trip in Africa, although they both spent far more time shooting pictures than guns that trip. They did, though, come back home and take up target shooting for a while, planning on going back with their "guns blazing this time" they joked.

When she told him she was pregnant, he tried to be excited but he hadn't wanted children.

"We never outgrow our childhood," he told her when they were dating, "no matter how far away we move or how often we change our phone number. What is it that Nietzsche says? 'When we are tired, we are attacked by ideas we conquered long ago.' The past is always lurking around the corner, waiting for that moment when your defenses are down." He looked at his plate and then up at Nicole. "All I know about raising children, I learned from my parents, and I'm not sure I want to be changing stinky diapers and fending off all those repressed memories at the same time."

Two months into her pregnancy, though, Nathan found himself getting used to the idea, gaining some confidence that the past didn't have to be "prologue to the present as Wild Bill Shakespeare wrote," he told her one night touching her stomach. Approaching parenthood much like he would a new class or a research problem, he read about what to expect and focused on creating a map for the future, a "baby syllabus" he joked.

The first trimester had gone well, but she started spotting one afternoon during the fourth month. The doctor sent her to bed "as a precaution. We can never be too careful." At around 2 a.m. Saturday, she woke up cramping, the spots now bright red. By the time they got to the emergency room, she was bleeding heavily and they both knew to prepare for the worst.

Nicole seemed to recover much more quickly than Nathan. In one of their follow up visits, his questions to the doctor grew so demanding she asked him to leave the room. Nothing seemed to satisfy his anger.

"We did everything right," he told her. "Diet, vitamins, exercise—everything by the book and your answer is basically you have no idea what happened?" He looked at Nicole for support, but she stared at him like he was a stranger.

When she came out of the doctor's office, she had pamphlets for some local support groups. Nathan dropped them in the dumpster the next morning on his way to the office.

A Head acts as a liaison between the faculty, students, and administrators. He represents his faculty by supporting their research and teaching while also enforcing high academic standards. Suspending a student for poor grades or disciplining a faculty member must be done fairly and judiciously, unless the person in trouble has a great rack and a nice ass.

It's like having job letter turrets or something, Nathan thought. Of course, pretty people do make a campus look more inviting.

"How come the students pictured on the web page are never in my class," Nathan asked a colleague at a departmental party last semester. "Do we have some stable of hot coeds who do nothing but walk around campus and pose?"

Shortly after Nicole left, one of Nathan's students invited him to her graduation party. "You've been a big part of my success, and I was hoping you would stop by and meet my parents. You're the reason I became an

English major." It wasn't the first time he had met a student's parents, but it was the first time a student asked if wanted to meet her "and some of my friends at the Steel Penny Pub in a couple hours?"

Later that night when they were in bed, she told Nathan she had been waiting for this moment. "God. You don't know how many times I would dream about you at night. The only way this would have been better is if you could have been talking about Flaubert the whole time."

Late one Thursday the next fall semester, June Moore knocked on his door. She had been hired as Department Head the year before Nicole left. She and Nathan started on the tenure track the same year, and they had both applied for the position. When the Dean told him June would be hired, he did his best to distance himself as the decision-maker, implying that the department, colleagues Nathan once respected, had spoken convincingly in favor of June.

Shortly after the decision, she stopped by Nathan's office to "make sure we're okay." Since then, she had "relied" on Nathan's experience and his "good judgment," but Nathan was pretty sure the Dean had told her to reach out and make sure he wouldn't cause any problems.

She had a troubled look on her face.

"Nathan. Do you have a minute?" She stood at the door.

"Sure, June. What's on your mind?" Nathan waved to a chair.

"We've known each other a long time, and you know I'm prone to speaking my mind so forgive me if I'm blunt." Even so, she hesitated and then held up a folder. "I've been reviewing everyone's teaching evaluations and reading student comments."

She opened the folder. Nathan sat there, hands behind his head, wondering how long they would keep up this charade. He was pretty sure June didn't even like him that much.

"This is a little bit awkward, but I wanted to talk to you about a couple of these comments before I passed them on to the peer review committee." June looked up and handed the folder to Nathan. "I put the relevant ones on top."

He noticed June looking at him and saw that it was his folder. Nathan flipped through the first three evaluations:

"Dr. Dumbrowski is a pretty good teacher, but he kind of creeps me out. He'll walk around the class and stand behind all the girls looking down their shirts."

"Dr. Dumbrowski used to be my favorite professor, but he's different. If you're his favorite—ie. a pretty girl—and stop by his office for a 'conference' you get an A."

"Dr. D is GREAT. And so sexy. Wink. Wink. I'll take his class (and anything else he's got) anytime."

Nathan read through the other evaluations. Another student accused him of playing favorites, and one wrote he was "pretty sure that's not coffee in Dr. D's coffee cup." The rest were banal, proving in some ironic way, Nathan noted, how clueless and apathetic most students are these days.

"You can imagine why I'm disturbed." She held her hand out for the folder. "These comments... well, we can't ignore them. I have to add, Nathan, that I've also been hearing some concerns from members of the department. Comments you've made, late night meetings with students with your door shut. Rumors, I'm sure, but, we have to remember that perception can be reality." She stood up. "I'll have to put something in a memo for the Dean, and I suspect he'll insist we look into this," she held the folder up, "more completely." She stopped and turned before leaving his office. "I'm a little worried Nathan, but I hope there's nothing to this. I know you've been going through some personal issues with Nicole leaving, but we can't cross that boundary and date students. If any of this is true..."

Nathan started to interrupt but June held her hand up.

"I stopped by as a courtesy because we've known each other so long. I don't think we should talk about it or get into explanations yet. I didn't want you to get blind-sided." She left his office and he watched her walk down the hall.

Well, technically June, he said under his breath, I'm not *dating* any of them.

Shortly after this meeting, and before the peer review committee met, Nathan started looking at job ads. He turned back to his computer.

Supporting faculty does not mean, however, that a Head will be able to please all of his colleagues. While a Head must live by a code that first does no harm, he must also be willing to lead faculty both by example and with clearly articulated expectations for performance. To get good head—

Nathan sighed. I'm either applying for a job or writing a letter to *Playboy*. "To be a good Head," he corrected.

He wasn't worried about an inquiry. While Nathan could be fired for moral turpitude, he was convinced there weren't a lot of morals around campus. The Dean was married to an ex-student, and it was well known that Troy Hill, the university's Nobel winning scientist, hired only female lab assistants after an extensive "interview" at his cabin near the lake. Bill Taylor held off campus "film and study" sessions in his advanced Anatomy and Physiology section, and Tony Dicicco met his graduate American novels class at The Library, a bar near campus, for their final. Any student who could drink him under the table got an A.

Above all, the Department Head must recognize his moral and ethical responsibility to his colleagues and, most importantly, the students. Knowledge is power and with that power, as Peter Parker's grandfather says, comes great responsibility. A Department Head must do the right thing not because there is a great reward, but because intrinsically we are helping our students become better people.

Nathan stopped typing and watched the cursor blink a few times and then looked at the clock. 5:30. The halls were deserted, and he got up and closed his door before pulling a bottle of whiskey from the bottom drawer. He had poured a small amount into his coffee cup when there was a knock. He took a quick drink.

"Come in." The door opened slowly.

"Professor Dumbrowski?"

Nathan could see a student poking her head through the partially open door.

"Are you . . . are you busy?"

"Come on in Jessica." Nathan turned in his chair to face the door. "What can I do for you?"

"I..." She stammered and Nathan could see she was nervous. With good reason, he thought. Jessica was failing his freshman composition class. How, Nathan thought earlier in the semester, she ever graduated from high school was beyond him. She rarely talked in class, and if truth be told, looked lost. In many ways, she was exactly the kind of student he would have worked closely with in past semesters, but this was the first time she had been to see him.

"What can I do for you, Jessica?"

"It's just. Well... I'm not doing real good in your class, and if I fail I'll lose my scholarship." She looked down. She had on a short skirt and a t-shirt, and she kept trying to pull the skirt down a little. Nathan waited.

"Well. Some of the girls in the dorms were talking and they said... they said you would work with students who weren't doing very good." She said the last words quickly and at a whisper. She looked up and stared at something over his head. "And I really need to pass this class and..." Her voice broke a little. "I guess I wondered if there was anything I could do, maybe..." She looked at him.

Nathan smiled to set her mind at ease.

"Come on in," Nathan said. "And shut the door so we don't get interrupted."

Later that evening, Nathan opened the job letter on his home computer.

The primary responsibility of a Department Head must be, by necessity, setting an example for appropriate professional and personal behavior in all his interactions.

Even when students are desperate, Nathan almost typed.

Nathan went to the kitchen and made a drink. He carried the bottle back to his desk and thought of Jessica leaving his office, her t-shirt only partially tucked into her skirt, one sandal strap flapping loosely across the top of her foot, but with an A in the grade book. He saw her stumble a little as she reached the end of the hall. Before she turned the corner, Nathan saw her straighten the hem of her skirt and bend down to tighten her sandal. She stood and Nathan could see her shoulders shake as a sob wracked her body. He looked back to his computer, his image on the screen distorted and fragmented.

Nathan took another drink. My god but you have become a lecherous old bastard, he thought. He closed his eyes and pictured Jessica's face as she pulled her t-shirt over her head. She had tears in her eyes as he lifted the hem of her skirt above her hips, putting one hand on her ass while he unclasped her bra with the other.

Nathan licked his lips and opened the bottom drawer of his desk, almost ashamed of the tingling in his groin. There was a box of shells and a small, Ruger .22 pistol he had forgotten about until three weeks after Nicole left. He had moved it downstairs while he decided if he would keep the gun or sell it. Nathan looked into the drawer and thought about Erica, Jessica, and other students waiting for their end of semester grades. He started to reach for the gun and then saw his brief case out of the corner of his eye, and he pushed the drawer shut, wondering if there were any other students struggling in his class and if they were good looking, desperate, and willing to conference after hours.

Hands on the Wheel

I first met Jolly when I was 15. My dad wasn't real happy when we started running together, but he never said anything—not directly anyway. Jolly is one of the many things I've realized over the years my dad got right.

I was sitting in a bar outside of Abilene, watching the Dallas news when the story broke. Police had found three black men, two shot and one stabbed, at a southside car wash/laundry mat. Early speculation was a drug deal gone bad, and the lead suspect was Jolly Henderson. The news showed a grainy surveillance photo on one side of the screen with a black and white mug shot on the other. I was working as a framer for one of those build them quick home companies, and my hands were cut and calloused in ways that would disappoint my father but afforded me some measure of respect in a place like this. It was 9:30 and I was hot, tired, and normally able to ignore the bad news that invariably signaled the end of another day.

"I been knowing Jolly for about five years now."

The guy on t.v. was a large, toothy man with a scraggly looking beard. He looked like that actor who always plays the fat biker—he's mean and tough but too ugly to have any lines. There were good reasons to keep him silent.

"His name was sort of ironical, if you know what I mean. I've not ever seen the man smile." The guy was enjoying his five minutes of fame. "Hell, he was just flat out a mean as a snake, if you ask me." He looked behind him toward the run-down shotgun house. "Still, I never figured him for nothing like this."

127

That's because you haven't known him long enough, I thought. I took a swallow of my beer and nodded to the bartender. The news anchor moved on to a doomsday story about food poisoning in salmon, and I slid a ten across the bar.

"Anyone who will spend that much on a piece of damn fish deserves to get sick." The bartender set my beer down. "If it don't taste good fried, I'm not sure you should eat it."

It was an observation, not a conversation starter. I smiled and he moved back to his stool. This wasn't the kind of place where words mattered all that much. My dad spent his life roofing other people's houses, frustrated that half his crew couldn't speak English and the other half didn't have anything worth saying. The older I got, the more I respected men who knew enough to be quiet.

The last time I saw Jolly was at my father's funeral. I was a junior history major in college and living on my own. The cancer hit hard and fast. Diagnosed in February, my dad was dead by semester's end. It wasn't much of a service. Me, the priest, and a couple of professional mourners— old school Catholic women with holy beads worn thin from use. My father was one of only a few permanent workers in a transient profession, and he was nothing more than 250 dollars a month at the trailer park. My mother had been gone since I was four, and my dad's family was never a topic of discussion.

"When I'm gone," my dad used to say, "that past won't really exist. I'm not sure that's such a bad thing."

He worked 10 hour days, only to come home and fight the encroaching apathy that poverty too often produces. Beer cans, broken whiskey bottles, and cigarette butts: the emptied evidence of diversions that help those down on their luck stay there and forget they might never leave. Trailer park yard art that shows up even in the neatest of yards.

When I graduated from high school, my dad handed me a bank book that had almost $8,000 in it. College money, he called it. "The best hand cream out there, son." His own hands were gnarled and nicked, maps of disrepair and abuse. Stained with tar and shingles. Hands that I wish I could still feel on my shoulder when times got tough, but hands he hid in his pockets when we visited Sam Houston State University the summer after I graduated high school.

* * *

Toward the end of the service, I noticed Jolly at the back of the church. He followed us to the cemetery in a beat up Pontiac Grand Am with rusted fenders and dents on both doors. I could see him leaning against the hood smoking during the ceremony. I thanked Father MacDonald and handed him an envelope—a small donation for the local homeless shelter. Cancer treatment isn't cheap, even when it doesn't work. By the end, there wasn't much left of him or his money, and I was pretty sure I had given the priest the rest of my tuition fund. It wasn't something I was worried about.

I walked toward Jolly. Slouched and pale against the cemetery's unnaturally green backdrop, he looked like a character from a bad rap video—Vanilla Ice dressed like Dr. Dre. I hadn't seen him since I left for college.

"Yo, Mikey. My man." He shook my hand and pulled me close like we were living on the street, ganged up brothers meeting before a deal. "Sorry to hear about your old man."

We stepped apart. I didn't say anything and Jolly looked down and then over my right shoulder.

"I know you're still pissed about the truck and all, but that's yesterday's news, man." Jolly slid his hands into his back pockets. "Back in the day, man, we were pretty tight. Your dad was righteous with me, and I wanted to pay some respects. That's all." Jolly looked at me for the first time and held up his hands, palms out toward my chest. His fingers were nicotine stained and there were scabs around his fingernails and on the tops of his hands. The tattoos didn't hide the tracks on his arms very well.

He was right, I guess. I met Jolly when I was fifteen, and he moved into the trailer across the way. One Friday night about midnight, Jolly tapped on my window. My dad was asleep, recovering from a week twelve feet closer than any man should be to a relentless Texas sun. When I was little, he would set a glass of milk in the refrigerator and bowl of cereal covered with Saran Wrap on the counter every Friday night. Saturday morning I could watch all the cartoons I wanted as long as I was quiet. A teetotaler most of the time, he ended his work week with a six pack of Coors before racking up fifteen hours of sleep in a pitch black room. He woke in time for lunch. We had a system.

The Friday Jolly tapped on the window, there was no glass of milk in the fridge. Long past needing my dad to pre-fix my breakfast, I still respected his need for sleep. Jolly had been in the trailer park for about a month, and we had hit it off pretty good. Jolly's childhood in the heart of Houston seemed pretty exciting. His father was in prison and his mother had relocated, carrying her problems into our neighborhood. Without my own relatives, I loved to hear Jolly talk about uncles who were pimps and aunts who were hookers. Men and women, it seemed, with tender hearts toward a boy but stone cold when outsiders showed up. I opened my window that midnight and stuck my head out.

"Jolly. Man. What the hell." I hissed, worried and nervous.

I hadn't ever snuck out before. It's not that I was scared, but I hadn't ever seen the need. My dad wasn't one to lecture, and we spent many an evening in relative silence around the house. Looking back, I can only remember a handful of times he spanked me. I know I was no angel growing up, but even as a kid, I would watch him come home with dried sweat around his collar and know he didn't need any extra work. When I did something wrong, he told me not to do it again. Quietly. With a strength unspoken and a hand on my shoulder. And it was those hands that reminded me how hard he worked. I tried to be the kind of son he needed.

But I was fifteen and Jolly was cool and kind of a bad ass, full of dangerous promise. I crept to my bedroom door, heard my father's slow breathing, and slid out the window. Jolly started walking down the street before I hit the ground. He flicked his cigarette, and I watched its arc until it bounced into the grass.

"Jolly. I gotta get back in the house. What's up?"

He didn't stop until we were near the end of the dead end lane. Farthest away from the community dumpster and filled with itinerant renters, the yards back here were littered with weeds trailer high and decorated with beer cans rusting in cockleburs and dirt.

Jolly lit another cigarette.

"It's cool." He put his hand on my shoulder. "Didn't you say your dad sleeps until noon? There's a party over at Bill Nutter's tonight. I talked Freddy into picking me up about 12:30, and I thought you might want to come along. We'll cut through the woods here and come up behind Smitty's." Jolly's hands were soft and thin, and I could see small burns across the back of his right hand.

"I can't go to a party, man. Goddamn. Sneakin' out... I don't know." I looked back toward my trailer, trying to talk myself out of heading down a path I knew I shouldn't take. "Your mom's gonna be pissed if she finds you out this late."

Jolly shrugged. "My mom's out. What she don't know won't hurt her," he said with a matter of factness that seemed sad even at the time. "Look, man, he's only going to wait a few minutes. You're either in or out, dude."

After what happened a few years later, I wondered how much might have changed if I had turned around and crawled back in my window.

My dad had let me take some sips from his beer the summer before, but one Friday night a couple of weeks before Jolly tapped on the window, he gave me my own can while we watched Sugar Ray Leonard defend his middleweight title.

"It feels good right now," he said, "and you might think you're pretty cool, but remember that no one ever found any real answers at the bottom of a beer can." He never took his eyes off the television, and I didn't reach for another beer. "Look at that man bob and weave."

He was right. It did feel good and I recaptured that buzz pretty quick at the party. Jolly kept bringing me little cups of beer from the keg, and around 3 a.m., Missy Kruger and I found a quiet place behind the garage. I was finally figuring out what to do with my hands when I felt someone grabbing my shoulder. Missy pushed against my chest, and I turned around.

"Dude. Freddy's leaving."

My tongue felt too numb to say much. Jolly laughed and put his arm around my shoulder. "Sorry, man." We started walking. "Plenty of parties this year and little Missy will be at them all."

I'm not saying I sulked all the way home, but I do know I was more focused on my hand sliding up Missy's stomach and onto her bra than what might happen at home. When I stumbled through the window, my dad was standing by my bed. I could see his eyes shining in the glow of the hallway light, and I thought of Jolly's cigarette flipping through the darkness. I started to open my mouth when his hand reached out. One blow. No words. I can still feel the calluses as they raked across my lips. The warm, nickel flavored blood trickled inside my mouth, and my father walked to the window and closed it. He stood there, arms across his chest, watching Jolly go inside his trailer. My dad turned and I closed my eyes, bracing for another blow. He put his hand on my shoulder. I could feel the power in his thick fingers: years of lifting shingles hadn't prepared him for a gentle touch.

"A man doesn't sneak in and out of a house. If you can't come in through the front door, don't walk in at all."

Time moves quickly when you're in a drunken slumber. I'd been asleep two hours when he roused me from the bed. Saturday morning was for sleeping, but by 8 a.m. we had mowed and edged the yard. The neighbors also paid for my delinquent behavior. By 10:30, I was on the trailer roof putting tar on bolts and cracks that were already sealed tighter than "a virgin's pussy" as Jolly might have put it at the time. My dad made sure I had water, and he let me take breaks when my stomach flip flopped, but I didn't get to linger long. I had finished vomiting shortly after 9 a.m., hadn't dry heaved in a while, and I had sworn off beer forever by 10:00. My lips were cracked and bleeding, but neither one of us mentioned the previous night.

Missy and I hooked up at future parties, and my vow against beer lasted about as long as most promises 15-year olds make. Jolly and I continued to hitch rides to parties, but when we were 16 and Jolly got his license, we rode together in his mom's car. My dad told me he was saving up, but we would have to share a vehicle for another year before he could get me something of my own.

I didn't sneak out anymore, though. I spent the night at various friends' houses, sometimes with Jolly, often with Freddy or Bill Mickelson. My dad didn't ask where I was going, but he usually told me to be careful. Any guilt I might have felt was gone after the first couple of beers. It was a tenuous morality, but one that made sense at that age.

Jolly's life took a turn, though. He was a couple weeks older than me, and the day after his 17th birthday, we both watched his mother carried away in a police car. He stood in the doorway, smoking a cigarette, trying to act like he didn't care. I sat in lawn chair at the far end of the porch.

A policeman came over, glanced at me, and then turned to Jolly. He asked if he needed to call Jolly's father or another relative to let them know what happened. Jolly looked at the policeman and then out at his mother in the backseat of the cruiser. He flipped the cigarette into the yard and walked inside the trailer. The policeman watched the cigarette burn for a little bit and then turned to me.

"Tell your friend I'll be seeing him again soon." He put his hand on the butt of his gun. "If I'se you, I'd find a different porch to hang out on. Your old man's good people. I'd hate to have to visit him and deliver bad news." He turned and walked back to the car.

Jolly's mom had her head back on the seat, asleep, passed out—didn't matter to her. It was another car ride. I could see my dad standing on our porch with his hands in his back pockets. Our eyes met. He shook his head and went inside.

A few weeks after Jolly's mom got arrested, my father and I went looking for a second car. He owned a 1970 Chevy truck with a little over 120,000 miles on it. We had spent plenty of Sundays changing the oil, rotating tires, checking belts. It was a truck you could still work on under the shade tree, but my dad said he was plumb tired of nursing it through the week. One Saturday we drove down to All-American Chevrolet, and he drove off the lot in a brand new Silverado. Metallic grey, cloth seats and a cassette tape player. He paid cash back when people still did that sort of thing. When we got home, we celebrated with some steaks and a couple of cold beers.

About the time we pulled the meat off the grill, we watched Jolly leave in his mom's rusted, two-door '72 Cutlass Supreme. The car was, or had been anyway, dark blue with an old small-block 350 and had a pretty serious hole in the tail pipe. I'm sure there was a time when that V8 ran smooth, but those times had long since passed. Everyone in the neighborhood was getting used to the backfiring coming and going at all hours. He raised his hand on the way by the trailer, and I could see him looking at the new truck. I nodded back, feeling drunk on my dad's happiness. I had plans to hook up with Jolly and Freddy later that night in the Safeway parking lot, but I didn't know if I would go. Jolly had been running with a different crowd lately. Guys a little older, girls a little wilder. These were people who drank fast and hard like it was a contest to see who could forget the day first.

"That boy looks as beat down as that car he's driving."

I turned to see my dad looking across the street.

"I can't remember the last time he didn't look rode hard and put up wet." He turned to go inside. I followed, wondering when, or if, he had ever even mentioned Jolly before. As we ate, my dad looked out at his new truck, and I didn't think about Jolly, or Freddy, or going out that night.

"Sometimes it feels good to own something new." He poured some steak sauce onto his plate, picked up his fork and pointed out the window. "I remember when I bought that truck of yours."

I watched him and ate.

"You take care of something and it should last a long time." He dipped his steak into his sauce and took a bite. He looked at me while he chewed and locked his eyes on mine. "Sometimes things get old and beat up but they're worth keeping because they still have some use."

He took a drink, looked out the window, and then back at me. I had stopped chewing.

"But when anything starts to cost more than it offers in return... Well, it's time to haul it out to the alley and let someone carry it off." We didn't say much for the rest of the meal.

I knew he wasn't talking about that old truck of his, but I didn't want to think about it all that much. I was 17, making good grades in school and having good times outside it. I had my share of drunken weekends, smoked a little dope, but mostly I cruised parties to have fun and avoided doing anything stupid enough to get arrested. I'm not sure I could always walk through the front door proudly, but I could at least walk through the door.

Jolly was a different story. He stopped going to school sometime in the fall. His mom spent time in and out of jail but that September she just "up and gone" he told me one night. The only real difference was that there were fewer police cars in the neighborhood after she left. Somehow, Jolly managed to pay rent for a few months, but one Saturday near Christmas, my dad and I watched the landlord empty the trailer. I still saw Jolly on occasion after that, but I knew by then he was dealing and, I'll admit it, I wasn't sure our friendship kept me all that safe from him or his life.

The Friday night after graduation I bounced from party to party. My dad had shown me the bank book that morning, and I can still see his hands shaking a little. Until that day, I couldn't tell people I was going to college, but that night I was making plans. My friends and I were talking about parties we would have, football games—the future laid out in drunken schemes of glory.

The lights were on at the house when I pulled in at midnight, but I didn't think that much about it. My dad had taken to falling asleep on the couch lately, his legs a little too sore from crawling up a ladder. When I opened the door, he was sitting at the table, a small rag on his knuckles. Without a word, I followed his eyes to Jolly on the couch, leaning back with a bloody rag on his nose, his earring partially torn from the lobe—he looked rode hard, but no one had put him up yet. His eyes were empty, floating toward the ceiling. I looked back to my dad and walked into the room. The t.v.'s slow hum kept time with the refrigerator cycling on and off. One of Jolly's teeth was on the carpet next to my dad's keys, but I didn't move to pick up either one.

"Your friend here needs a ride." My dad broke the silence as I leaned against the wall. He took the rag off his hand, and I could see new scratches etched on his knuckles. "I caught him headin' toward the door with my keys." As he spoke, my dad stood up and picked up his keys and Jolly's tooth.

"I think you should call the cops, dad." I moved forward, took the tooth, and started walking toward the couch. Jolly stood, rag off his nose, looking like a cornered animal. My dad put his hand on my arm, and I felt his strength through my shirt. My mind's eye saw me finishing what my dad started. My dad tightened his grip.

"Michael. I said he needs a ride."

I turned and my dad shook his head.

"If you can't take him home, or somewhere, then I will. Once you decide something costs more than it's worth, you got to leave it and walk away."

Jolly and I didn't talk. I should have taken him to the emergency room. His nose was bent sideways, and his breath was ragged. I got into town and dropped him at the bus station. At the time, I thought I was being pretty clever, but for a good long time after that night, I couldn't shake the image of his eyes as they dulled and his hand half raised as I pulled away leaving him alone and in the dark at the station. I was one more person driving off while he stood alone without a ride.

* * *

Even at the funeral, I wasn't all that interested in catching up with Jolly. I appreciated that he came, and I'm still not sure how my dad had treated him right. I guess Jolly respected my dad's power and his willingness to handle the break in without police. It wouldn't have mattered. He was headed down that path long before he moved anywhere near us. Trailer parks don't make people trashy, but they can sure attract trashy people, my dad said one Saturday morning when we were working in the yard.

My dad's college money was gone after the funeral, and I dropped out. I tried a semester working and taking classes, but I couldn't ever make ends meet in class or at the bank. My dad worked hard to keep me from having to struggle like him, and I realize that his yard work wasn't about keeping up appearances. Lord knows his hands needed the weekend off, but he knew that you have to keep the grass cut and the trash picked up or it will creep right into the house.

I finished my drink and raised my hand to the bartender. Stepping outside, I could feel the first hint of autumn creeping into the air, and I knew that the construction work would start to slow with winter. There weren't many cars in the parking lot, and I could see the light reflecting off the metallic gray of my dad's old truck. Every once in a while, on nights when the past comes creeping in to the present, I can sit in the cab and imagine him next to me.

I opened the door and put my hands on the wheel. My cracked knuckles and scarred fingers were easy to see despite the darkness all around me. As I sat there in the truck breathing the cool air, I thought of Jolly and I figured it was time to walk away one more time. I suspect I'll start back to school once the work gives out, but when I do, I'll lay my hands out on the desk and let people read whatever story they can find in the cuts and calluses I've earned since last time I was there.

The Petting Zoo

Christie leaned back, trying to melt into the couch cushions, wishing she could wake up when her kids where 18 and in college. She smelled strawberry and felt the sticky residue of a half finished Jolly Rancher on her neck as she cradled the phone against her ear and tried to concentrate. The ceiling fan was filthy, there were spider webs in three corners, and she had at least one couch cushion poking her in the thigh, but she wasn't all that sure what her husband had just said. Her ability to have an adult conversation was in direct proportion to how well her children behaved on any given day.

"What? Sorry. I just spaced out for a minute. How can there be spider webs but no spiders?" Christie leaned to the side. If she couldn't feel the spring, maybe she could pretend it wasn't broken. "Anyway. You weren't there. I've never been so embarrassed in my life." She listened to Simon talk, wondering why her glass of wine was so far away. And how it got empty.

"I think we've been banned from the petting zoo. For life. Our grandkids won't be able to go either." Christie forced herself to stand. She needed a drink more than she needed rest. Or, more likely, she needed the drink in order to rest. The Jolly Rancher smell followed her to the kitchen and she wondered if there were any good snacks left.

"I'm fine. Just trying to get off the couch. Alexas told me at breakfast she wanted to grow up to be a kangaroo so she and David used the couch as their own personal trampoline this morning. I was outside watering plants for less than five minutes. When I came in, they had grocery bags tied around their waists with a small stuffed animal in each bag. They were yelling 'Boing, boing' as they hopped from cushion to cushion. Our couch looks like that hideous, plaid sofa you had in college. I don't know what's sagging worse—me or it."

Thankfully, the wine bottle was still on the counter. She wasn't sure she had the energy to open the refrigerator at this point.

"It's easy for you to tell me not to feel bad. You didn't watch your daughter eat the animal food out of the vending machine today. She kept telling me, and anyone else who would listen, she was eating the animal crackers." She heard Simon laugh. "Trust me. It's not as cute as it sounds."

She poured the wine in her glass not quite ready to tell the whole story.

"I dropped her off at mom's house on the way home. David's there, too. You need to stop by and pick them up on your way home." She took a small sip while he asked a question. "No. I decided not to take him. I thought it might be nice if it was just us girls. Plus I was worried he might act up. I should have taken him and left her. Listen, Simon, I'm pretty tired and I want to rest a little before the kids get home." Christie started to put the phone down and saw the bottle of wine on the counter. "Simon, are you there?... I'm taking this bottle to the bathtub, and you're bringing pizza home for supper. No rush. Trust me, she ate like a pig today. Literally." Christie laughed at her own joke and wondered if she should take two bottles with her.

She was in the bathtub when Simon got home and came into the bedroom to change. Even with the bathroom door closed, she could hear Alexas singing, and knowing Simon, David was asleep on the couch. She was ready to shoot Old McDonald, all his animals, and whoever wrote that damn song. A veritable farmyard massacre. She slid under the water, tying to maintain the illusion of peace and tranquility, but Calgon had lost its power.

"'The world is too much with us.'" She let a little air out of her mouth. "Unbelievable. A bachelors degree in English and I can't remember who wrote that line. At least I know every word to a thousand nursery rhymes," she thought as she raised her head above the water.

"I'm still in here," she called out when Simon knocked. "I'll be there in a few minutes. You guys go ahead and eat. And don't let David sleep anymore. He'll be up all night."

Christie picked up her wine glass. "To motherhood." She raised the glass in a private toast. As she stood, she saw her reflection in the mirror. Two babies down and four more to go if Simon gets his wish. She straightened her shoulders then turned sideways, pushing her chest out and sucking in her stomach trying to reverse gravity.

She was sitting on the makeup stool crying when Simon knocked again.

"Pizza's on the table. David's asking where you are. Are you okay?"

Christie unrolled some toilet paper and wiped her eyes. "Just drying off. Be there in a minute." She stood and looked in the mirror again.

When Simon climbed in bed later that night, she could tell he wasn't interested in going to sleep right away. Christie thought about telling him her head hurt or she was cramping. He might huff and sigh for a little while, but she knew he would keep his hands, and the rest of his body, to himself.

It was one of the reasons she loved him and why she felt a little guilty when she avoided sex. Before she got married, her older sister and her mother both told her the key to a happy marriage rested on lying: "on your back and when it's over."

She and Simon laughed about their advice, but the older she got and after two children in three years, she was starting to change her mind. Still, Christie thought as Simon put his hand across her stomach, sex with Simon had never been a chore. He was gentle and focused on her. Even as she felt less and less attractive, his desire for her seemed to stay strong. "Especially, tonight," she thought as he moved up against her.

Afterwards, and after Simon fell asleep, Christie lay awake listening to the house creak and the wind blow outside. In some ways, these were her favorite hours of the day even if she would pay for it in the morning if Alexas came bounding in the room "bright eyed and bushy tailed" as her mother might say. Lying there, though, Christie kept replaying the petting zoo disaster that afternoon.

"It wasn't so much the crackers or trying to climb on the lamb's back," Christie told Simon after the kids were in bed. "I knew it was time to leave when she starting pointing at the donkeys and asking 'Can I smack the ass, mommy?'"

Simon let out a little snort.

"I had no idea what she was talking about until she asked if Shrek and Princess Fiona were there. When I told her it was time to leave, she grabbed the rabbit cage and wouldn't let go." Christie made her hands into two fists clenching invisible bars. "She wrapped those tiny little fingers around the wire. No screaming, no yelling. She hadn't been quiet the whole time we were there."

Simon, to his credit, put his hands in front of his smile.

"And of course, the place is packed. It's like national take your child to the petting zoo day or something and I didn't know what to do. All the other kids were acting normal." Christie could feel the weight of the day pushing down on her all over again. "I tried to talk to her, and I know we said we would never bribe our children, but that was before one of them got a death grip on a rabbit cage. I offered her anything I could think of. Ice cream, a stuffed animal, cookies, but she shook that little head and grabbed the cage harder. The petting zoo worker, this big burly guy who's mad he can't work at the real zoo, came over and told us we needed to leave. 'Ma'm, your daughter is scaring the rabbits.'" Christie laughed at herself but there was no real humor in it.

Simon sat down next to her on the couch. "I'm sure it wasn't that bad." He put his arm around her shoulder.

"But it was, Simon." She was fighting back tears. "I had to pry her fingers off the bars, and when I did she started screaming. All these other mothers were looking at me. Once I got her loose and we were finally leaving, she started yelling 'I want to stay here forever.' And of course, I see Margot Addison and her three kids." Christie paused and took a deep breath. "Three perfect little girls, dressed in these matching outfits and walking out the gate, happy, smiling, and doing exactly what they're told. I've got one daughter and she's wearing two different colored socks with hair that looks like she was raised by wild animals." Christie rested her head on Simon's arm and closed her eyes. "After we got in the car, she sniffled once and asked, as if the last ten minutes never happened, 'Can I have my ice cream now?' God. I can't teach my kids how to behave in public, and I can't even bribe them the right way."

Simon pulled her closer, and she was thankful for the quiet.

The phone woke Christie the next morning at 7:15. Simon was already in the shower and David and Alexas were still asleep.

"Good morning." Betty, Simon's mom, was always so cheery first thing in the morning. "Did I wake you, honey?" Betty didn't wait for an answer. "Silly question, I know. I'm sure you're getting breakfast ready."

Christie felt like hanging up. Instead, she did her best to sound as awake as possible for someone with three hours sleep.

"Good morning Betty. I'm up. You caught me with my hands full already." Christie lied, sitting up in bed.

"Oh, good. Although, I'm surprised those kids are up already. I heard Alexas had a big day at the petting zoo yesterday?"

Christie closed her eyes and held the phone away from her ear, offering a silent scream to the world.

"All her questions are rhetorical," Simon told her after Christie met her the first time. "In some ways, a conversation with my mom is relaxing because you don't have to say anything or listen too closely. I promise—she already has an answer to any question she might ask you."

When they first started dating, Christie wanted to like Simon's mother. Betty was always so full of energy and there were no dull moments. She got up every morning with her husband, made him breakfast, and left the house when he did. Active in the community and her church, she was home by 3:00 to start supper. On the weekends, she cleaned house, top to bottom.

Each night, Simon told Christie, his mom would tell everyone all about her day. "Every detail. Or, at least, every detail that involved her saving someone's day from ruin. It was always important that we knew how much she did for the world and at what sacrifice." Simon called it her martyr complex. "She'll eat burnt toast, too. She fancies herself a kind of Mother Teresa minus the vow of poverty or the humility."

Christie, on the other hand, spent half the morning in her bath robe, getting out of bed after the kids woke her up. She asked Simon, after Alexas was born and they decided she would be a stay-at-home mom, if it bothered him being alone in the mornings before work.

"I love my mom, but my god she never shuts up. One of my greatest days in college was when I realized I could drink coffee in peace."

Simon came out of the bathroom. Christie looked at him and rolled her eyes. He shrugged his shoulders in apology and left the room with what Christie hoped was a sympathetic look but was, more likely, a sense of relief he hadn't answered the phone instead of her.

"Well, Alexas did enjoy herself." Christie found over the years that the best way to get off the phone with Betty was to offer as little information as possible.

"I talked to Julie Hogan last night. She was there with her grandkids, and she mentioned, in passing of course, that Alexas got a little excited when it was time to leave." Betty paused. "I'm sure you were frazzled, too."

Christie could tell Betty was fishing for details. When Alexas was born, Betty was always there with what Simon called her "free advice." At first, Christie didn't understand his cynicism, but seven years of marriage and two children later, she was learning to listen selectively.

"You know, I'm sure dear, that the key to raising a precocious child like Alexas is to help her with coping strategies. When Simon was a child, he was always so smart he would..."

Christie zoned out.

Simon walked back into the room with a cup of coffee. He set it on the night stand and put his hands around his neck as if he were being hanged. Christie stifled a little laugh.

"What was that dear?"

"Nothing, Betty. Simon was telling me he needed to leave." She gave him a mock serious look and shooed him out.

"Well. I wonder why Alexas was so upset? She was over-stimulated, I'm sure. You have to monitor her because she's so sensitive to changes in her routine. Our children were so mature at four and five. They knew before we ever left the house the kind of behavior we expected, and I honestly can't remember any public displays. The tantrum, and I know I don't have to tell you, is never about the..."

Christie would offer small signs she was still on the phone, but she closed her eyes and tried to enjoy her coffee while it was hot.

Simon warned her the first time she met his mother that it was best to "never, never, ask a question. Treat her like you would a crazy person on the street. You might throw a dollar in the can, but do not engage. No eye contact. Let her talk until the tape winds down."

Alexas walked in the room and crawled under the covers, snuggling up near Christie. Hard to believe this was the same hell-child who traumatized rabbits yesterday, Christie thought as she put her arm around her daughter and pulled her closer.

"Betty. I'm sorry to interrupt, but Alexas is getting hungry. I appreciate the advice. It's always nice to talk to someone who's been there before. I'll let Simon know you called." Christie counted to 214 before Betty hung up.

Christie finished her coffee before she and Alexas got up and went into the kitchen. Simon was putting some papers in his briefcase.

"My mom help you out and solve all our parenting problems?"

"Soon, if we're lucky, we'll have kids almost as perfect as you were as a child." Christie poured another cup of coffee. "My god, Simon. She must think I'm an awful mother."

Simon came over and gave her a hug.

"I know you told me not to listen to her, but she said we are supposed to teach Alexas coping strategies and talk to her this morning about what happened yesterday."

Simon stepped back from Christie and turned to Alexas. "Alexas honey. Why didn't you want to leave the petting zoo yesterday?"

Alexas glanced over her spoon at Simon. "I was having fun, daddy. And mommy was being mean." She put the spoon in her mouth.

"How was mommy being mean?"

"I was playing with the animals and she made me leave when I didn't want to." Milk dribbled down her chin as she talked.

"Are you supposed to do what mommy says?"

Alexas looked at him and then at Christie. She nodded and Christie could see her thinking, deciding if this was a trap of some kind.

"Did you do what mommy said yesterday?"

"Yes."

"Really? You left the petting zoo when mommy said it was time to go?"

"Yes. Mommy even bought me ice cream for being such a good girl."

Christie laughed out loud and she saw Simon smile. He turned to Christie. "She's training for law school." He looked back at Alexas.

"Did you do what mommy said without crying and yelling or scaring the rabbits?"

Alexas hesitated before answering. "No but I wanted to stay there forever and I want to move to the petting zoo and have a rabbit and turtle and little horses for pets."

They could see she was getting upset, and Simon walked over and gave her a hug, tickling her ribs as he let go of her. He put his jacket on and picked up his briefcase.

"There. Tell my mom we got to the root of the problem after hours of deep, psychological probing. Christie, remember that all my mom knows about parenting is from the rewritten narrative of our childhood and Dr. Spock. The only thing our daughter needs to cope with is being five."

When the kids went down for their nap, Christie called her mother.

"Thanks for taking care of the kids yesterday, mom. I'm sure Alexas filled you in on the petting zoo fiasco." Christie was sitting at the table eating a small salad. She was determined to lose a little weight and get back in shape before Simon was ready to start trying for baby number 3.

"The best part of parenthood," he called it. "We have sex and then you labor."

"You don't know what happened? Betty called me at 7:15 asking about it. I'm amazed Alexas didn't say anything when I dropped her off?" Christie took a bite and laughed at her mother's comment about Betty. Even though both sets of parents lived in town, they never became friends.

"They're your in-laws," Christie's dad told her the week before she got married. "You have to get along with them, not us."

Right after Christie and Simon were married, Christie's mom invited the whole group over for dinner. The next morning, Betty dropped by unannounced and offered Christie's mom "some recipes she might consider. Just some healthy alternatives," she had said.

"Man cannot live on vegetables alone," her dad told her mom. "The day I eat tofu and yogurt for supper, you might as well put me in a home."

"Alexas had a total meltdown at the petting zoo. I had to pry her fingers off the rabbit cage and then we were asked to leave."

Her mother laughed.

"It's not funny mom Betty called this morning to tell me I needed to 'dialogue' with Alexas, and she asked if I needed 'communication strategies.' Simon wants four more kids and I can't handle the two I've got." Christie had finished her salad but was still hungry. "And I'm getting fat, but I want to eat all the time. How did you keep it all together?"

When Christie got off the phone with her mother, she felt a little better.

"Betty raised five children so I'm sure she knows a lot, but your father and I always tried to keep things pretty simple. You know him." Her mother tried to imitate her father's voice. "Six million years of evolution. We don't need a bunch of darn psychologists telling us how to raise kids. Of course he didn't use the word darn." Her mother laughed a little. "Raising kids is hard but I'm not sure it requires coping strategies or dialoguing. Mostly you have to be patient and figure things out."

She heard her mother getting plates down from the cabinet. Her father would be home for lunch soon, and Christie knew she would have soup and sandwiches for him.

"The only thing Alexas needs from you is a hug. She's a little girl with her own strong mind and that takes a special kind of patience. She's a lot like you. With Susan, we would tell her something once and she was always so eager to please. Your dad had to be pretty tough on Tim, but he would eventually do what we wanted. But you. You had your own stubborn streak. When you were 11, you had a ten speed and you wanted to ride it every-where. In the summer, you asked if you could ride to the pool, but we wouldn't let you cross Fredericksburg Road."

Christie remembered. All her friends would meet at the pool to swim and visit, but mostly because Jimmy Salvatore was a life guard.

"You rode over there once and your dad told you if you did it again, we would lock the bike in the shed for a month."

She could hear her mother opening the refrigerator.

"The next day, right after your father left for work, you walked out the door with your swim bag and didn't come home until after 5:00. You came in and put the key to your bike lock on the table. 'I locked the bike in the shed,' you said and walked up to your room."

Christie smiled. She had been grounded for two weeks, but, even now she felt like reminding her mom she had been able to cross Fredericksburg Road safely. Christie heard the door open.

"Your dad's here for lunch, dear. Let me know when I can watch those babies again. They'll embarrass you now, but you can make it up to them when they're teenagers. Give our love to Simon and hug their necks when they get up."

After supper that night, Christie wrote out a list and went to the grocery store. She used to go during the day, but the last time she went with the kids, Alexas crawled under the cart, acting like a T-Rex, growling and snapping her hands at everyone's legs. David sat in the cart hiding under a 24-pack of toilet paper. She didn't think that much about it, she told Simon when he got home, until she noticed the store manager following her.

"I'm not sure I can handle the unpredictable nature of parenting," she told him. Christie started running more and more errands after the kids where in bed.

As she turned the corner out of the produce aisle, she saw Margot Addison and quickly looked down at her list, hoping she could feign distraction long enough to avoid the embarrassment of a conversation.

"Christie"

"Oh, hi Margot. I didn't see you there. So focused on the list and trying to get out of here at a decent hour." Christie held up the list and didn't quite stop the cart, wanting to seem busy enough to justify her anti-social behavior.

"Oh, I know. I hate shopping at night, but it's so much easier than coming during the day with the girls." She pulled next to Christie's cart. Christie stopped and leaned on the handle, trying not to look impatient.

"Well, your girls are always so well behaved. It can't be that hard." Christie hoped, too late of course, that she didn't sound bitter.

Margot laughed. "Last time I brought the girls, we abandoned the cart on aisle 22. By the time we got to the car, we were all in tears. Audrey had a moment near the frozen pizzas. Oh my god it was so embarrassing."

Christie smiled, surprised.

"Hey. They sell coffee over here. Do you want to get a cup? Todd's watching the girls and the grocery store is about the only private time I get anymore."

As they sat at one of the little pub tables the store installed about a year ago, Christie couldn't remember the last time she talked to another mother without children around.

"Did you guys like the petting zoo the other day?" Margot asked.

No wonder she never talked to other mothers. She gave a kind of noncommittal nod as she took a sip of her coffee.

"I had to laugh when I saw Alexas as you were leaving." Margot stopped. She closed her eyes and put her hand to her mouth and Christie heard her mutter a muffled "Oh my gosh."

She was about to get up and leave before Margot could offer her child-rearing advice. She didn't need another Betty in her life.

"I'm so sorry. I didn't mean it like that." Margot was talking quickly. "I wasn't laughing because Alexas was throwing a fit. I knew exactly how you must have felt."

Christie doubted that. "Your girls looked like perfect little angels yesterday."

Margot laughed. "That was dumb luck." She took a sip of her coffee. "We were at the petting zoo because I told Zoe I would take her if she got Audrey and Hope to behave. I'm not sure what she did, but I also don't care. What did one of my professors used to say, 'I like sausage but I don't want to know how it's made' or something like that. It had something to do with showing your work in a Calculus class. God. I used to remember things like that."

"I know how you feel. The other day I was trying to remember the author of a poem, and the only name I could think of was Dr. Seuss."

They both laughed. Christie could feel her shoulders relax.

"I'll bet Alexas got in the car and calmed right down, didn't she?"

"As if nothing happened. She even asked me for ice cream like she had been a perfect angel the whole time."

"That's priceless. Kids. Hope did the same kind of thing the other day. Two weeks ago she climbed up in the tube at McDonalds and wouldn't come down. We were out shopping for Todd's birthday present, and the kids had been so good at the mall I decided to treat them to a hamburger. I thought I could rest a little while they ran off some energy. Have you been to the new McDonalds?" Christie shook her head. She couldn't decide what was more surprising: Margot's kids sounding like Alexas or picturing them at McDonalds.

"Well, they have these new tubes. They're 15 or 20 feet high and the slide comes down into this giant pit of balls. Todd doesn't like it because he thinks the pit is full of germs. Plus, he saw some *Dateline* special or something where rattle snakes could nest in the pits. I told him when he stayed home with three girls under ten he could decide how to fill the day. Until then, I wish McDonalds had a wine menu." Both women took a sip of coffee.

"Everything was going fine," Margot continued. "The kids had eaten. They'd been running up and down the tubes and I told them they could go one more time. Afterwards, Zoe and Audrey climbed out and walked over to the table. We all waited for Hope. A couple more kids came out of the tube but still no Hope." Margot smiled a little. "That seems like a strangely prophetic way of saying it doesn't it? Anyway. I finally stood up because I was ready to go. Audrey needed a nap and I'd had all the greasy, fast food smell I could take. I looked up and Hope was sitting at the top of the highest tube. Just sitting there. I waved at her, motioning for her to come down and she waved back, smiling big as you please. After a few seconds she moved to the top of the slide and stopped. By now, there's a traffic jam of kids sitting behind her. I called out her name, trying not to yell but she acted like she couldn't hear me. Everyone in McDonalds probably thought she was slow or deaf. And god knows what they thought of my mothering skills." Margot took a sip and Christie put her hand over her mouth to hide the smile.

"Oh. It's okay to laugh, but it gets better. She wouldn't move, kids were piling up behind her, my face, I'm sure, turned a Ronald McDonald shade of red. The other two girls were getting fidgety. Zoe kept asking why Hope got to keep playing, and Audrey needed the bathroom. The other mothers were starting to look at me so I did the only thing that made sense at the time and climbed into the ball pit, stood at the bottom of the slide, telling her to slide down. I was trying to yell without yelling, if you know what I mean. Somehow my mom knew how to pull that off so well. Hope grinned at me. She knew I wasn't going to do anything to her in public. God. Todd and I don't spank our children, but I've started reconsidering lately." Margot smiled and shook her head.

"How did you get her down?"

"Oh. When I watched Alexas with that iron grip on the rabbit cage yesterday I thought how lucky you were. At least you could reach her. I started to climb up the slide. Thank god I wore shorts instead of a skirt, but it can't have been a pretty sight. Three kids and fifteen years ago, maybe

148

the teen age boys working behind the counter would have enjoyed the show. Nowadays, I'm on my knees, crawling up the tube, wishing I had eaten a McSalad instead of chicken nuggets, wondering if I'll even fit in the tube. I've got my backside stuck out for the world to see, and I heard this kid. 'M'am. M'am. You can't play on the equipment. It's for children.'"

Christie choked a little on her sip of coffee.

"I turned and sat down, looking over at Zoe and Audrey. Zoe was walking toward the entrance to the tubes so she could keep playing like Hope, and Audrey was dancing around letting me, and everyone else, know that she was about to pee in her pants. Hope was still sitting at the top of the slide watching me, smiling like she was having the time of her life. There were about ten kids behind her waiting patiently and every mother in the room was thanking God or Buddha or any deity they could think of that they weren't me and this pimply-faced, squeaky-voiced teenager thought I was trying to climb up the slide so I can fly into the pit of balls like I'm eight. I gave him this look that let him know I was about to go on a murderous rampage, and he started taking some steps backwards. 'M'am. Do you need the manager?' Right as I stepped off the slide, Hope flew into the pit. I climbed out with whatever last shreds of dignity I had left, went home, and sent Todd an email telling him I was putting our children up for adoption."

Christie wiped tears from her eyes. "Oh my god. I'm sorry I'm laughing so hard. She climbed out like it was no big deal, didn't she?"

"Oh yeah. She even asked this morning if we could go to McDonald's for lunch today. I didn't have the heart to tell her our pictures are probably hanging on the wall next to the top ten most wanted, the hot check writers, and the Hamburglar. I told Todd we were going to have to change her name from Hope to Despair as fair warning to everyone who meets her."

When Christie got home the kids were already in bed. She told Simon the story over a glass of wine.

"I guess everyone, even people named Todd and Margot, have their petting zoo moments as parents. Sounds like you two will have to get together more often since your kids are getting thrown out of every place in town."

That night, when Simon put his hand on her stomach, she rolled over to him, happy to meet him half way.

About a week later, Alexas and David asked if they could go to the petting zoo. David hadn't been yet and they had been watching something on the Discovery Channel about rabbits. Christie looked at Alexas standing by the kitchen table. One red sock was down by her ankle, and she had a blue sock pulled high on her calf. David was in a t-shirt and his pajama bottoms but he had on cowboy boots.

"I'm a pig farmer," he said when Christie asked.

Between swallows of milk, they were singing Old McDonald. Christie shook her head, knowing she was going to regret saying yes. Maybe they won't remember us, she thought as the kids climbed in the car. When they got to the petting zoo, she stood in front of David and put his cap on his head.

"David. You're my rock. I know you'll behave, but remember: no jumping, be gentle with the animals, and don't run off."

She wasn't worried about him. David was far more cautious than Alexas. She turned to her daughter.

"Alexas, I know you're excited, honey, but I need you to hold my hand and remember our rules of good behavior." Christie held up a finger. "What's rule number 1?"

"No climbing on the animals and number 2." She held up two fingers. "Do what mommy says." Alexas beamed, proud of herself. Christie smiled.

"That's my girl. We can't have a repeat of our last visit to the petting zoo, right?"

"I'll try mommy," she said, "but I can't make any promises."

Christie pulled both children close, whispering that she loved them. I guess I can be happy with that, she thought as they walked through the gate and toward the rabbit cages.